Hands

The chord swelled upward, blissfully, rising in pitch and timbre and encompassing me. It was such a grand noise, blocking out every other sound. And the music bid me to do what was mine to do.

I closed my eyes and slowly reached out my hands. I could feel the music now, encouraging me, and I gently gripped the injured leg in my tiny fingers, careful to do no more harm.

A voice spoke behind the music, more puzzled than angry.

"David? David?"

The music kept me focused, more in control than I could possibly be, and I let it come. I gave the dog the music, feeling the chord as it moved down my arms and through my hands. The music whispered comfort as it flowed, bathing me in warmth and the inner glow of unseen light.

The music left gradually, drifting away in vaporous mist, so I did not feel emptied all at once.

I woke to my surroundings, the rain still drenching me, my breath filled with water, the cold upon my skin—feeling incredibly alive.

The little dog gingerly tested the leg. It worked. He cocked its head at me and then bounded into my lap, licking my face until I giggled aloud. After a moment I put him down, and he scampered away on four whole legs.

What They Are Saying About
Hands

"There is a moment when the reader is so absorbed that the pages disappear and all that remains in the story playing itself out in one's head. That is the sign of true storytelling: when the book itself evaporates. With Hands, Street has accomplished that."

Gail Gabrielson
The Forum

Wings

HANDS

by

M. A. Street

A Wings ePress, Inc.

Paranormal Romance Novel

Wings ePress, Inc.

Edited by: Karen Babcock
Copy Edited by: Leslie Hodges
Senior Editor: Karen Babcock
Executive Editor: Marilyn Kapp
Cover Artist: Kathy Williams

All rights reserved

Names, characters and incidents depicted in this book are products of the author's imagination or are used fictitiously. Any resemblance to actual events, locales, organizations, or persons, living or dead, is entirely coincidental and beyond the intent of the author or the publisher.

No part of this book may be reproduced or transmitted in any form or by any means, electronic or mechanical, including photocopying, recording, or by any information storage and retrieval system, without permission in writing from the publisher.

Wings ePress Books
http://www.wings-press.com

Copyright © 2010 by Mike Unrue
ISBN: 978-1-59705-601-4

Published In the United States Of America

September 2010

Wings ePress Inc.
403 Wallace Court
Richmond, KY 40475

Dedication

For Donna

One

I remember the first time I heard the music. I was only four then, but I remember every sound and shadow of that day. The day the music became my life. The day that is impossible to forget.

I remember how confused I was. Nothing in my room could have made the sound. I searched the rest of the upstairs without success. I hurried downstairs. My mother, a piano teacher, was off in the kitchen, and her piano stood silent. The television and radio sat mute.

The only other sound was the gentle rattling of pans as my mother fixed supper. She smiled broadly at me as I stuck my head through the doorway.

"What is it, honey?"

"That music," I said.

She listened. "What music?"

"Don't you hear it?"

She stilled her hands and listened again. "I don't hear anything, David. Must be somebody outside. Why don't you play for a little while, and I'll call you when supper's ready."

Then she smiled again, and the music stopped, seeming to evaporate into the steam that rose from the pot simmering on the stove.

After so many years and so much history, I still find the music difficult to describe. It always begins the same way, a thin, muted sound, like a distant trumpet. The single tone grows louder, and more sounds join in: brass, woodwinds, bells, chimes high and low, all playing the same note, advancing into a rippling effect.

The sounds waver and waft as if on air, as if every invisible particle shimmers in the light and joins in symphony.

Then the note splits into a single chord, growing in intensity more than sheer volume, the way sunlight glares through a window even when the air outside is freezing.

The chord moves into a crescendo within a few seconds, rising and signaling a change to come, growing ever louder. And then...

The chord broadens and surges upward into such sweetness that to hear it replaces all notions of heaven—or the chord falls into chaos, an oppressively loud and painful racket, as if every player was struck down at the same moment.

The difference is far more than mere esthetics. The difference is lethal.

We lived near Glendale, California, in what had once been tract housing built following the Second World War. All the houses on our street were nearly identical when built. Only time and the gradual machinations of the people who lived there distinguished one from the other.

Some had stuccoed the exterior. Others had enclosed the small front porches. Our next-door neighbor, Florence, my mother's best friend, had planted her entire yard in flowerbeds, separated by thin strips of grass. Our other neighbor had nursed an azalea hedge to a height of seven feet the entire length of our boundary.

In our house a front bay window had been added, and its window seat was my sanctuary. I'd spend hours sitting on a cushion, staring out into my world. Not that anything extraordinary ever happened there. It was simply a place that belonged to me.

One day I sat there watching a slow, steady summer rain waste the warmth of the day. My mother was playing across the room. I grew up with Bartok and Bach, Schumann and Chopin. The music from beneath my mother's hands always brought comfort.

A dog wandered into the yard. Not much of a dog, really, a cat-sized mutt of white and tan spots. But the dog favored a rear leg. So gingerly, in fact, when moving faster it picked up the rear leg and skittered along on three.

I watched, knowing intuitively something was wrong. And as I watched, the note came, the muted horn, the breathy woodwinds, quickly, all the same melancholy sound. The music tremored and rose like the wind in the trees, growing louder.

The chord came, beautiful and powerful, and I could feel it inside me, compelling me without understanding. All because of this little dog. I flew across the room, the chord ringing in my head.

Once outside I heard my mother call out as if from some distant place.

"David! What on earth, David, come back here!"

I walked straight to the dog, the rain soaking me to the skin, a slip of a boy in shorts and a T-shirt. My hair was glued to my head. I had to squint to see, even though I needed no sight at all. The music guided me, and nothing else seemed to matter. With every step the music grew, lifting me to a higher place even as it moved me forward.

The dog looked at me oddly but didn't run away. Somehow I believe he knew. I crouched beside him and ushered him closer. If I spoke, I don't remember. He simply limped over and stuck his head against my stomach. I knelt.

The chord swelled upward, blissfully, rising in pitch and timbre and encompassing me. It was such a grand noise, blocking out every other sound. And the music bid me to do what was mine to do.

I closed my eyes and slowly reached out my hands. I could feel the music now, encouraging me, and I gently gripped the injured leg in my tiny fingers, careful to do no more harm.

A voice spoke behind the music, more puzzled than angry.

"David? David?"

The music kept me focused, more in control than I could possibly be, and I let it come. I gave the dog the music, feeling the chord as it moved down my arms and through my hands. The music whispered comfort as it flowed, bathing me in warmth and the inner glow of unseen light.

The music left gradually, drifting away in vaporous mist, so I did not feel emptied all at once.

I woke to my surroundings, the rain still drenching me, my breath filled with water, the cold upon my skin—feeling incredibly alive.

The little dog gingerly tested the leg. It worked. He cocked its head at me and then bounded into my lap, licking my face until I giggled aloud. After a moment I put him down, and he scampered away on four whole legs.

I turned and saw my mother standing there, a veil of doubt and a small reflection of fear on her face.

"I did it, Mama," I said. "Did you see?"

Her voice was so low I almost didn't hear her. "Yes, baby, I saw."

She reached for me and held me tightly, as if I might somehow escape her grasp. She held me for what seemed a long time before she let me go, the rain still pouring down on us.

"Let's get inside before you catch cold," she said finally, and carried me to the house.

She said nothing about what had happened, and I began to feel I'd done something wrong. But the music didn't return, and I began to think less about it until the day became like the rain that had passed into fog and night.

~ * ~

A couple of weeks later we drove into town. We had black wrought-iron columns on our porch, and she was tired of the color.

I always enjoyed walking with my mother. She never walked too fast or hurried me along. She held my hand most of the time, but let go when I wanted. She never made me feel I was in the way.

She stopped in front of a department store window to look. She had a weakness for summer dresses, and I remember how pretty they looked on her, the hem flowing as she moved, the soft patterns and pastel tones a reflection of her natural warmth.

For me to think of Margaret O'Beirne as young was impossible then. My mother was not even thirty-five years old, and later I was able to appreciate just how beautiful she was with slender legs and long fingers, and hair the red of autumn sunset. She was in her prime, something incomprehensible to me.

As we stood there a man moved by, his right leg in a cast. I was fascinated: how he swept his crutches forward in unison, swung his body through and planted his good foot, gliding ahead. Still, I knew something was unnatural about it.

The tone began, distant and dull, soon ushering in the rest in ritual preparation. So I welcomed it. I knew why the music came. I slipped free from my mother's grip and followed after him.

He was still much quicker than I, and soon I was running after him as fast as my short legs would carry me. The chord rose, growing, waiting even as I chased him. I felt that ecstatic upward turn even before it happened. The feeling was there and I knew what it meant, and I loved the sensation. I was closing the distance, my hands outstretched in anticipation...then suddenly found myself airborne and swung backward.

And the music died like the slamming of a door.

She carried me silently all the way to the car. The worried look on her face scared me. She drove away quickly. The car lurched and the tires squealed, and her expression did not change, and I wanted to cry without knowing why. All the way home she did not utter a word.

That feeling lasted into the night. She toweled my hair until my scalp was raw, stuffed me into my pajamas, and jerked the covers over me. Finally, the tears began to flow.

"What'd I do?" I whispered.

She looked at me and touched my cheek with a trace of a smile. She sat beside me.

"Don't cry, baby."

"Why are you mad at me?"

"I'm not mad at you. You didn't do anything wrong. I'm sorry if I made you feel that way."

I breathed with relief. "Okay."

She waited until I had settled in before speaking again. "Do you know what you can do?" she asked gently.

I shook my head. Suddenly I didn't want to talk about it.

"You make hurt things better," she answered for me.

I shrugged.

"Do you know how you make hurt things better?"

I didn't answer. I sneaked my hands from beneath the covers and wiggled my fingers.

She grinned at my gesture. "Yes. With your hands. Do you know how special that is?"

"No."

"Well, it's very special."

I was confused. "Doctors do what I do."

She sighed and brushed the bangs from my forehead. "No, David, they don't. They use machines and medicine, but they can't do what you do."

"You mean they don't hear the music?"

"No, they don't hear the music. I don't hear the music. I don't think anyone else in the whole world hears the music the way you do."

I still didn't understand, but the idea was delicious. "Would I be famous?"

Her smile drooped a little. "Too famous, honey. That's why I think we should keep it a secret, just between us. Would that be okay?"

I nodded. She began to caress me then, and spoke very softly. "We live in a big world, David, and one of the things I've learned is no matter how much we see, or how much we think we know, there is always something more out there. And sometimes, every so often, something happens to show us that, even though we don't always understand it at the time."

"I don't understand it, Mama."

"I know, baby. Maybe someday you will. But for now, maybe that's not the important thing. Maybe the important thing is to see the good it can do, and to believe the reason it's here in the first place is to do good."

"I want to do good," I said.

She kissed me. "Then you will."

I wasn't so afraid any more. I should have been. But that night, as the music came and went in my dreams, I slept peacefully.

~ * ~

I had been to the Valley Nursing Home on many occasions. My mother volunteered there. She played piano in the big open room they had, and the old people sang.

I didn't like the nursing home much. I had no inkling what being old really meant, but the home was full of people with wrinkles and gray hair, crooked backs and toothless smiles, and who spoke gibberish some of the time as they wandered aimlessly. And the whole place always had a funny smell.

Once inside my mother pulled me into a corner where no one else could hear. I could sense a kind of raw excitement in her above the muffled noise.

"You remember what I told you about old Mrs. Aynor," she said.

"I remember."

"She's sick with something called diabetes, and they think she might lose one of her legs."

I nodded. I really didn't have a clue. I only knew Mrs. Aynor was important to my mother. "I'll try."

She rubbed my shoulder. "Good. She's asleep now. She won't even know you're there. I'll stand right outside the door and make sure nobody else comes in. I'll be there the whole time."

"Okay."

"Okay, then."

She led me to the door, and I looked in. The room was dark, and all I saw was this lump lying motionless in the bed. I looked at my mother. She gave me a nod of encouragement. I went inside.

The room smelled rotten, and I wanted to turn around. My mother pulled the door part of the way closed, which made the room even darker, littered with ghosts who stood watch but did not move a muscle. I looked back and saw her standing guard, but I was still scared.

I moved to the bed. Mrs. Aynor lay curled up into a ball with only the top of her head and the part of her hand that gripped the blanket showing, as if already dead.

But nothing happened. The music didn't come, and I didn't know what to do. I touched the tip of her hand. It was icy cold. I shivered and looked around, utterly lost. I wanted to go home.

Then some of the ghosts came into view. Framed pictures on her nightstand—pictures of children, one about my age. I didn't know who they were, but I knew they were the people who loved Mrs. Aynor, the people Mrs. Aynor loved—the people who would miss her if something happened.

Almost like a prayer—I'm not even sure I said it aloud—I called *come*.

The note came. The notes in flight. Then the chord, faster than ever before, taking me by surprise, the upward motion soaring skyward so quickly it left me fuzzy in the pit of my stomach. I reached trembling hands toward her, the music continuing to rise as if to match me inch-by-inch, movement-by-movement.

I gently gripped the cold flesh of her hand. She didn't move. I closed my eyes. I gave the music away, feeling it flow in the same rush in which it had come. And the more I gave her, the more power filled me, until the music surrounded us both like the heat of deep summer, though ever in silent darkness. I didn't want to let go.

~ * ~

We didn't speak until we were well on our way home. She bit her lower lip, waiting.

"She's well, Mama," I said finally.

She sighed aloud but said nothing. And when I looked again tears sparkled in her eyes.

"Are you okay?"

She smiled. "I'm fine, baby." After a few moments, she glanced over at me. "You will have so much magic in your life, David. You will know what it's like to be truly blessed."

I settled back. I wish time had frozen for us, that we'd never had to move beyond that moment. She didn't know how wrong she was. Eventually, she would know. Not all, of course, but enough.

Two

All those who knew Mrs. Aynor had prayed for such a deliverance, and when it came no one doubted and no one wondered.

My mother saw to it that I was never long out of practice. At least once a week she would take me to some place where I could do what I did, and do it undetected.

Old people who would fall asleep in chairs or on benches. A boy whose asthma was so bad he couldn't even go to school, but whose mother brought him out on warm, clear days to nap in the fresh air. Those unconscious from drink or drugs, some sleeping in alleys.

I didn't have even the slightest connection to any of them. Sometimes we would drive for hours.

My mother kept me away from doctors and hospitals. Away from people who were watched all the time, or whose sudden recoveries would have aroused too much attention. This really began to bother me, when I would see someone ravaged by the effects of cancer or AIDS, or who bore the horrendous scars of fire or accident, or had some birth defect. For these I could only look, and then couldn't stand to look long.

Sometimes I would not have the energy to continue. The music was stronger than I was, a burgeoning capacity

I could not comprehend, though still locked in the weightless soul of a child. And when the burden would get to the point where I could not bear it any longer, or the music would exhaust me and the tears would inevitably come, my mother would stop and find other things for us to do together. I was still a kid, a child of the times, perhaps—a child of awareness beyond my years, but also my mother's son.

Soon, however, I would do what was in my power to do. The music never stopped, never let me ignore it for long, never ceased to remind me what it was. A constant presence.

~ * ~

To describe the other as merely a harsh or painful noise would not do the sound justice. And since it is inside my head, would not do me justice either.

The beginning is always the same, no inkling of what is to come, no warning as to what will follow: the far-off note, followed by its company, like butterflies at wing, the chord strong and sure, always lifting...

Imagine then any major disruption: a thousand cars in gridlock, horns blaring; an orchestra composed of a hundred zealots, each feverishly playing a different part so to be heard above the rest, like mad children of Babel; the cries of the damned in the lower levels of Hell, each besting the other; the thunder of the world's destruction in ceaseless roar: all in unison, and surrounded by an electric wind capable of reaching into every nerve. A cacophony of violent clatter sufficient to rend the soul with no way to stop it...

That is a kiss compared to the way it feels.

When I was in the third grade I came home on a warm Indian summer afternoon to the familiar sound of some poor kid mangling Clementi or Bach, while my mother gave gentle corrections with infinite patience. I entered quietly and went into the kitchen.

I went straight to the refrigerator, and as if by magic, the mangling stopped the precise moment I opened the door.

"No snacking before supper," she called out. And the moment I closed the door the mangling resumed.

I sat out on the back stoop to let the sun beat down on me. I have come to believe we are not so different from plants. Light affects us the same way, nurturing us, and we atrophy in the darkness. I loved the neutral warmth of days like this, and I munched the apple I had snatched from the bowl on my way out, smiling to myself that I had managed to avoid her invisible alarm.

I wallowed in the light until a low, guttural growl from the back fence startled me. Then I saw the cat, inching across the yard, its haunches bloodied to exposed, raw flesh as it struggled toward our neighbor's house.

I tossed the apple aside and approached the cat, walking softly with my hands at my sides to show I meant no harm. It saw me and tried to hurry away, managing only to drag itself, mewling pitifully.

I circled back to head it off and crouched down, speaking as gently as I could.

"It's all right. I won't hurt you."

I picked him up gingerly, careful not to touch any of the wounds. They were disgusting, a runny one near its hip open to the muscle, its genitals perforated and swollen. The cat protested loudly and tried to wriggle free. I released my grip and cradled him loosely in my arms. He continued whining but stopped squirming.

So I hurried. The note, the accompanying host, coalesced into the chord. I placed my hand as near the hip wound as I could without touching it, awaiting that blissful upward turn—

The force of the ruckus that followed knocked me down. I flinched, and the cat screeched liked his ancestral beast and twisted hard with his claws extended. In one furious swipe he raked the back of my hand and I dropped him, while the noise hammered me senseless.

I covered my ears with my hands and staggered toward the door. The cat slunk away as quickly as his wounds would allow, and only then did the sound inside my head begin to subside. The blood began to ooze and flow down my fingers, the pain sharp and already throbbing. I hurried inside.

My mother held the hand over the bathroom sink, washing the cuts and daubing them with a cloth to stop the bleeding. The cloth was soaked, but the wounds were mainly superficial, a fact which seemed lost on her.

"I've warned Florence about that damn cat," she fumed. "She should've had it fixed a long time ago."

I had to say it. I needed to hear myself say it. "It didn't work."

"She shouldn't let him just roam around like that. Always getting into fights, getting into the trash, getting into my flower beds."

"And it's not the first time either."

The moment settled around us, and I knew she'd heard me because her treatment slowed and she glanced at me before resuming her care.

"There probably wasn't time," she said, reaching for the iodine.

Time had nothing to do with it. "A guy twisted his ankle at school," I said. "I knew it was bad, but nobody else did, so I got to him first without anybody paying much attention. He was shaking, and I nodded like I knew what to do. I loosened his shoe and pretended to give him first aid, you know, so after it was over he would think the sprain just wasn't as bad as he thought. It didn't work. And I knew it wasn't going to work."

She was digesting this. She shook her head a little as she dressed the scratches. "How did you know?"

"The music. It was different."

"How was it different?"

"Awful. Like it wasn't really music any more. Like the loudest noise I ever heard."

She watched me out of the corner of her eye. "Well, don't fret about it. It'll come back."

She put the last piece of tape in place. "All done," she said, with a gentle kiss on the bandage. "You'll live?"

I beamed at her. There was life with her, and no life without her. "I'll live."

She gave me a quick pat and began to rinse the sink. "It's nice to know I'm still good for something."

~ * ~

Wrongness had invaded my world and I couldn't deny it, as if the music itself wasn't unsettling enough. One night I dreamed I was lying on my back and couldn't move no matter how hard I tried. Several sets of hands hovered over my bed, glowing white and swaying back and forth, taunting me.

I'd learned I could conjure the music, and I began to do so many times a day. Always the same: the note, the flurry, the chord swelling. Then I would stop, pushing it back into its secret place, afraid to go on. At times the music would fight, the chord struggling against my will like a ship prow to the wind, but I had learned to focus on a single thought—No! No! No!

Still, I had to know. I sought out injured animals—creatures with no self-consciousness, or the type who, if they could sense anything at all, would sense I meant them no harm. It made no difference.

I looked within. If I could not feel genuine compassion and a conscious desire to do good, I would not make the attempt at all. Fast or slow, in all weather and environments, careful to remove every conscious obstacle, no doubt or fear or hesitation, I tried and failed.

I succeeded much more often than I failed, but I still had to live through a downward spiral of agonizing sound, and the failures wore on me like a weight fixed to my heart.

Young though I was, I felt the burden. This was not some external force. The healing music lived in me, and so came entirely from me. I didn't know how to make the music beautiful. I didn't know how to make it sing only its healing song. The music either did or it didn't.

My mother saw its effect on me. We would remain at some distance from someone or something, and I would invoke the music and wait until I knew its course before I moved. But at times even that didn't work. At times the music would suspend itself until I ventured closer, seeming to encourage me, until I actually placed my hands upon a soreness or wound, before shattering as if mocking me.

Failure became too much to bear.

~ * ~

Sheila Adams tormented me. She hid my books. She put spoiled fruit in my locker. She ambushed me with pine cones and howled with laughter when I ran away. And she left a note for me nearly every day saying how much she loved me.

Late in the school year I was walking home. I always enjoyed the walk, the insignificance of sounds that never seemed to change, the uniformity of trees planted thirty years before that gave our street a sense of time, the ambient comfort of the samenesses that seemed to favor or disfavor no one.

I didn't see her bearing down on me, the Christmas bike already worse for wear. She zipped along the sidewalk, ignoring everything in her path, a mad slalom that left people jumping and old Mr. Hill chasing after his hat in her wake.

She clipped my elbow, and my books flew in all directions. She whooped as she sped by.

"You're gonna get it, Sheila!" I shouted.

"You have to catch me first!"

She turned to look at me over her shoulder, her square nose wrinkled in challenge. She crossed a wide driveway that sloped steeply toward the street. The bike turned downward before she could face forward and right herself.

That's when I saw the oncoming car, and Sheila moving directly into its path.

"Look out!"

She showed nothing more than faint curiosity. I was already moving. I've heard that tragic things happen in slow motion, that you remember every detail. They don't. They happen in the blink of an eye, branding the impressions into your brain with swift and horrific clarity.

The driver did not see her until it was too late. For a brief moment a tree blocked my view and I hoped they had managed to avoid each other. Then I heard the brakes squeal and an empty thump.

In two strides I was clear. Sheila lay several feet away from her twisted bicycle. The driver, a young woman, had opened her car door and her mouth at the same time, her horror still breathless and silent.

I sprinted to them. Blood grew in a dark red halo beneath Sheila's head. I stopped and caught my breath, my first thought to run away, my second to stand there wringing my hands and bawling like the driver.

Instead I moved to her. In the distance my mother and Florence stood and talked in the yard, turning slowly toward the scene. They seemed to move in unison, and I heard the distant speaking of my name, a question, my mother wondering if the victim was me.

I knelt beside Sheila, my back to the driver. Her eyes were open but stared blankly into oblivion. She was still alive. I could hear her breath rattling in her throat, being forced up and through her mouth.

The driver's howl was an awful distraction, but I tried to block it out. I called the music. It came, the notes floating like dust motes looking for a place to light. The chord began, strong and sure. I pushed the power forward as I reached.

Disharmony rose like a blasting siren. I jerked my hands away. Still, the music raged a wicked storm inside my head.

I took a deep breath and pushed the noise back until there was only the chord, ceaselessly faithful and true to me. I felt a warm wetness on Sheila's cheeks. Blood. I felt a warm wetness on mine. Tears.

Come.

The chord dissolved into grief and pain and a roar of hateful racket. I withdrew my hands to make it stop. Now it wouldn't. The cacophony circled like a pack of wolves to keep me at bay, and I couldn't push it back.

From the corner of my eye I could see my mother and Florence arrive. Florence went to the driver, wrapping an arm around her and hissing in an effort to calm her.

Helplessly I looked at my mother. She knew something was wrong, but forced a slight smile and gave me a nod of encouragement.

I reached again, the clamor still there, raucous and raw and horrifying, lashing out as if to ward me off, but I didn't stop. I pressed my hands upon her face and tried to give the music away, hoping the sweet resonance would return, but it would not. My head began to throb in loud misery, and the noise held me insensible, blaring red until it engulfed me, overwhelmed me.

Suddenly the blaring stopped, and I realized I had been abruptly pushed aside, landing on my hands and knees. And there to replace the riotous blast was a cry of such anguish I didn't know which was worse.

Sheila's mother. She fell to Sheila's side and cradled her head in her lap.

"Oh God! My baby! My baby!"

My ears were still ringing as the more innocuous sounds of the day reclaimed the air around us: the pitched murmurs of gathered voices, car doors slamming, shuffling feet. Another sound called me then. Sheila began to gurgle, and thick red bubbles rose from her lips.

"No!" her mother wailed. "Call an ambulance! Hurry! *Hurry!*"

I looked to my mother for some shred of consolation, but she simply mirrored my pain and it was more than I could bear. I flew toward the house as fast as I could.

I sobbed in my bed. I heard her footsteps on the stairs. I tried to stifle my cries with my pillow, my ribs aching with every gulp of air.

She sat beside me, gently stroking my back. "David, honey, it's not your fault."

I sobbed harder.

"David, look at me."

I did, still quivering, still unable to catch my breath.

"It's not your fault. It has never been your fault. It's something out of your control."

I viciously shook my head and squeezed out the words. "Yes it is."

"No it isn't. Why in God's name would you even think that?"

"Because Sheila's gonna die, and I could've stopped it."

Tears welled in her eyes. I didn't remember ever seeing her in so much pain before. "No. You couldn't have stopped it."

I began to sob even harder. I gulped every breath, and even then it wasn't enough. Finally the truth spewed from me. "It's me, Mama. Don't you see? I tried to tell you before. Something in me keeps it from working. And now..."

I couldn't continue. The wracking sobs consumed me, and like the music, I let them take me, praying to forget all I had come to know. Finally I flung myself into my mother's arms.

"Oh, Mama, I just want it to go away."

I could feel her arms tighten about me, pulling me in. "I know, baby," she whispered. "So do I."

~ * ~

Later a strange calm came over me as I lay alone and listened. I heard the ambulance pull away and sensed the commotion in the neighborhood. I heard the phone ring once and knew the caller was Florence telling my mother Sheila Adams had died.

Lying in the darkness I knew what had to be done. The music was life and death, and death came far too easily. I summoned all my strength and with cold resolve I called the music to me. It came painlessly, almost apologetically. Then I pushed it back into the black void from which it had come.

Over and over, throughout that sleepless night, I did this. I called it to me and I let the chord rise, only to choke it off, banishing it to the more harmless fringes of my thought, until it not dare come again without my bidding—until all bidding ceased.

Three

The two of us had always lived on our own. I never knew my father. She had explained it as simply as if teaching me a C scale. "Your father was in the Navy. He was stationed all over the world. I met him here, and we fell in love without thinking about the consequences."

"What do you mean?"

"Well, he was stationed on an aircraft carrier. He couldn't stay in one place, and I didn't want to leave. Even if I had, we wouldn't have been together much. So we agreed that he would go and I would stay. The decision hurt us both very much."

"Did you have a fight?"

For a brief moment she looked transported to another place. "No, that's what was remarkable. Even in the end we still loved each other."

"And he just left."

"Yes. He went back to his life. And I had my life. Now we have our life, which is the most important thing in the world to me."

"So why doesn't he ever call or write or come to see us?"

She looked sad then, and for more reasons than she could tell me. "We thought it best not to complicate things. Right or wrong, that's what we decided." She looked at me intently. "You are the biggest part of my life. But when the time comes for you to be a part of his life, I promise you I will do everything I can to give you that chance. Okay?"

I nodded. I felt cheated, even though I didn't really know why. Sometimes a presence of any kind seems preferable to the absence of the unknown.

~ * ~

I was twelve years old when I found an old box of colored pencils. I was drawn to them like water to earth, happy to give my hands an occupation.

My mother had tried to teach me the piano. I learned the fundamentals, but much to her disappointment, I think, I just didn't have the knack. I loved Debussy, though. I loved to press the sustain pedal and hear the notes hanging in the space about me. I learned a couple of his pieces well.

Maggie said it was always all or nothing with me. I guess she was right.

I began drawing, first trying to duplicate the Sunday comics. Then I moved up to photographs, finally getting to the point where you could tell who or what the subject was.

That Christmas she bought me my first set of paints. I went through them in two days. I painted everything I could see, and I got better at it. She encouraged me and kept me in supplies, though I'm sure paying for them wasn't easy for her. I mowed lawns and did odd jobs to buy my own.

I learned two tricks early on. By making well-placed creases in the canvas, either with a thumbnail or the dull edge of a nail file, the paint would adhere better in those places, creating depth and highlights. If I layered the background first, usually with a wide brush, I could add contrast when I began working on the subject matter. I loved earth tones and darker shades, and I loved to capture any image frozen in time.

The music still haunted my sleep when I could do nothing. Afterward, I could not find release unless my hands were actually in contact with the oils. I would dip my fingers in, stroke the paint on, smooth it into place, working the pigments relentlessly. The process pacified me and also moved me into a new level of proficiency.

I took my first formal art class as a sophomore in high school. I was a source of frustration for Mrs. Jackson, my teacher, though my obstruction wasn't deliberate.

"You don't conform to traditional systems. You don't take direction, and you are wildly inconsistent," she would say. "But you have an amazing talent, David, perhaps even a gift."

One night about a year later the music invaded my sleep and woke me. The calling was especially persistent. The harder I tried to push the urge aside, the worse it got. Finally I got up and attacked a new canvas.

I decided to show the painting to Mrs. Jackson. I waited until after school when no one else was around. She held the canvas for a long time before placing it on an easel, then studied the painting even longer without expression or sound. I already knew to beware her kindness. Compliments were her way of encouraging a student who had no real skill whatsoever.

A trace of sadness crossed her face, an expression I'd become intimate with in my mother.

The painting was simple. The foreground was an enormous pair of disembodied hands, human yet glowing with an ethereal light. And in their shadows was the image of a boy, smaller, even insignificant, his face a blank, his eyes large and dark, his arms outstretched...and without hands.

"It would seem to indicate the struggle every artist experiences to control the uncontrollable," she said finally.

I said nothing.

She looked at me. "You know, the state competition is coming up. There is a bracket for your age group and an open bracket for all nonprofessionals. Could we enter this?"

"Would I have to be there?"

She frowned in understanding. "God forbid you should meet other artists, let people get to know you, even enjoy yourself."

"I just don't like having to explain anything," I said. "I'm no good at that."

"I know. But you worry me, young one. I worry you'll end up in a cave somewhere."

"Only if it had cable," I said.

She chuckled, but returned to the painting. This time she seemed fixed on a particular point, and I had no idea why.

"What's this?" she muttered. She retrieved a small magnifying glass to peer above the boy's head. "Wings? No, wait. Another set of hands."

I looked. At first all I saw were the familiar swirls that appeared in everything I'd ever done. Then I looked through the glass. Amid the cumulus of oils was the faint outline of a pair of hands reaching skyward. The placement was purely unintentional, but there they were.

She turned to me again. "Clever."

"It was an accident."

"No," she said. "It's a signature."

I won my age bracket and finished third in the open bracket. Mrs. Jackson even got an offer to buy the painting. I wouldn't sell. Instead I kept it hidden in the attic with the rest of my stuff. The medals, I hung on the wall to satisfy my mother.

Mrs. Jackson did bring me to the attention of colleges, and I began to get letters asking me to apply. I didn't know what good attending art school would do me. I didn't think I could ever make a living as an artist, and I didn't have the patience, disposition, or desire to teach, but the attention was all very flattering. I began to apply.

~ * ~

I stood beneath a tree in the blue-gray haze of an early spring morning. The air was crisp. The ground was alive with color, my breath fresh and cool. I recognized her immediately—older, like me, but very much the same with that boxy nose and crooked, devilish grin. Her curly brown hair had straightened somewhat, she no longer wore those ever-present glasses; and the freckles had completely vanished except for a light spray across her nose, but I knew her.

"Sheila," I whispered. "You look great."

"I've missed you, too," she said.

I reached for her hand. She withdrew it at first. I understood. Then she grinned mischievously and touched me. I placed a hand atop hers.

Shock crossed her face the same instant I felt the warmth. I lowered my gaze. Blood covered my fingers. But not her blood. Mine, flowing from my hand. I recoiled and wiped it on her shoulder. A deep red stain appeared on her white dress.

Stunned, she asked, "Why did you touch me?"

I tried to stop myself, but something was terribly wrong. I couldn't stop touching her. Everywhere I touched became soaked with blood, and I was helpless to stem the flood.

She began to back away in horror. I followed, desperate to rid myself of pestilence. I swiped at her with every step, wide swaths covering her. She kept retreating, but I kept stalking her. I grabbed her with both hands, blood spewing everywhere. She kept retreating but not quickly enough. She was nearly covered.

Again and again she cried, "Why did you touch me? Why did you touch me? Why did you touch me?"

"David! David!"

I was trembling, my arms outstretched and flailing, still trying to rid my hands of corruption.

"*David!*"

I awoke in a stupor. My mother gripped my shoulders firmly, shaking me. The dim light of the attic showed my hands and arms covered in red. I focused—a familiar smell—paint. And there on a canvas before me were incoherent streaks of crimson.

Frantic worry marked her face. "Are you all right?"

I took a deep breath, regaining my bearings. "Had a nightmare. Sorry."

"I know, baby," she said. She hadn't called me that in years. She pulled me close. "I know."

~ * ~

I was two weeks shy of my eighteenth birthday when the letter arrived offering me a full scholarship to the University at California at Berkeley. I thought I would be a wreck. Quite the contrary, the prospect of being in a new environment, to begin anew with no identity at all, was exhilarating.

Mrs. Jackson was thrilled for me. Margaret Rollins O'Beirne was not.

I stood packing in my room, early in August. I could feel her in the doorway without looking. I didn't have to look to know she had aged. She was barely fifty, but gray hair framed her face before retreating into auburn, deep lines had gathered at the corners of her eyes, and she was never without her reading glasses.

I could not fathom the serenity about her, a faith in the ultimate goodness of things, and that her humor had not diminished with the passage or weather of time. I had no great understanding of the depths of love. But all the love I had was hers. She had kept me safe—she had kept my secrets.

I smiled to myself but did not look. "You think I need an audience?"

She stood in the doorway, arms folded. "I can't believe you did this."

I looked at her. "Did what?"

"Grew up on me."

We both smiled. "Couldn't be helped. Besides, I'm not really leaving. Just going to school."

She moved closer. "No, this will always be home. But things will be different now."

"Well, at least I won't be underfoot."

"I'll miss that most of all, Scarecrow."

I dumped the contents of my sock drawer on the bed, many I had never worn. "Just don't send me any more socks."

She came and sat on the edge of the bed, watching me. "Only if you grant me a small indulgence."

"Speech time," I teased. "Been saving it, have you?"

She smiled, resignation in the curve of her lips. "Well, it's just that I know you don't want to hear it."

I looked away. She was right. I was hoping to avoid this conversation, but I'd known it was coming. Suddenly I was nervous and began to busy my hands.

She stopped me and bade me to sit beside her. "I honored your decision. I knew how hard it was for you at times, and I tried to be there for you, but I didn't try to influence you."

"I know. And I always appreciated it."

"Well, we both know it's still there, David. It hasn't really gone anywhere."

I shook my head. "It's better this way."

"Is it?"

God, I hated this. "You know it is."

"I know it has caused you great pain."

I could feel the bitterness churn inside me and the tension in my neck, and I didn't want this to happen, not now. I looked at her pleadingly. "I like who I am, Mom. I'm not always happy, but I want to have a life. I want to do things."

"You will, David. Everyone knows you've got what it takes to be an artist."

"Then why not just let it be?"

"Because it's a part of you."

"So what?"

She paused. "I'm not doing a very good job at this, am I? I guess what I'm trying to say is this. I believe inside every person are the pieces of another person, no matter how deep or buried they are. His best self. It's the same for everyone, not just you. And sometimes I think that's the real key to happiness. To let that person evolve. To let that best self be."

"What makes you think I can't be that now?"

"Maybe you can. But you can't ignore that something very powerful lives in you. Something that just doesn't happen very often."

I didn't answer for a long time, and even then I couldn't bear the whole truth. "It's not the same as it used to be. I don't even think it works anymore."

She studied me, but there was no challenge in her voice. "Then so be it. But promise me something, David. If you ever have to consider that your best self somehow involves this thing, don't hide from it. Do whatever you can to make peace with it."

Long before I had entered the realm of invisible sorrow, where unseen clouds descend to mix with the free air, to rob life of its perfect breath.

Ignorance and neglect had been my only salvation, however scant and incomplete. I wasn't going to change that now.

"David?" she said gently.

I smiled to put her at ease. "I promise.

Four

I was lucky in college. I didn't have to take calculus or economics or biology or political science or psychology. I studied art: art history, form and function, composition, media.

And what I learned first and foremost is that the value of some art is not in the arrogance of being one of the few who understands it, or pretends to understand it—art that requires an opinion as to its art-ness—but in being one of the masses who look upon something and share the soul's recognition, in whatever portion, of some element of perfection.

That connection is racial, as if fixed in our genetic code, and spiritual in calling to whatever meager particle of divinity is inherent in us. And the shared appreciation is evident in each of us the moment we are exposed to it.

The sparse use of color in Botticelli's *Primavera* and his understanding of anatomy and perspective mean nothing to those who simply recognize love. That Rubens' *St. George Slaying the Dragon* was done with pen and simple brown ink is less remarkable than that there is valor in all of us, however remote. Rembrandt perfected the group portrait in *The Night Watch*, but the knowledge that during the same time three of his four children died in infancy and he lost his wife soon afterward is what reaches us. And what speaks to the devotee in the radical use of color in Matisse's *Green Stripe* would without explanation speak to the simplest of us that he adored his wife.

I was incapable of such greatness, but I would rather produce a single speck accessible to that elemental part in all of us than a world of complexity comprehensible only to a few.

I worked. It was wonderful. I painted every day and had access to nearly limitless resources. I learned portraiture and proportion, and an attention to detail that came easily to me. I developed colors and hues obsessively, cataloguing every tint and blush I ever created or encountered, duplicating hundreds in a book I created with canvas pages that soon became too heavy to carry, and then duplicated most of these on several different surfaces.

The instruction was excellent and impersonal, which satisfied me all the more, and I soaked knowledge up like a sponge. I began to move away from all I had known before. My freshman year I came home a half-dozen times, Christmas, and the entire summer. By the end of my sophomore year I was only coming home for holidays. My mother teased me about it, but I could see the hurt in her. I began to avoid that, too, knowing I did not have the power to heal the pain of our separation.

Then there was the music. My mother had been right. My gift really hadn't gone anywhere. Sometimes the note and the chord would lie dormant for a long time only to rise when I was most vulnerable, leaving me even more so.

I made no close friends, but I learned a valuable lesson I didn't really like; that entire relationships could be built and maintained with virtually nothing of substance exchanged. A kind word was still kind whether it had any real depth or not; a touch was still a touch whether there was real affection behind it or not.

I went out with April Laws a few times. A fellow art student, April considered herself an outcast. She wore baggy clothes with sandals and never shaved her legs or armpits. She was a great welder, and I used to tease her that if art didn't work out for her she could make a fortune in a body shop. When I knew her she was working on a collection of sculpture where she took the hoods of old cars and attached mannequins to them in various provocative poses, like bizarre hood ornaments.

I lost my virginity to her. I remember the music twisting like a summer storm inside my head, but I learned to touch and caress in spite of that. It was difficult, often impossible. The more I reached out emotionally, the worse the music became, but I swore to myself that I would learn to love.

The world was full of pain, and any time I encountered suffering the music would come as a warning, whether the damage was a skinned knee or a serious accident. I could not avoid these imbalances, temporary or permanent, so I tried to view them as normal, small adjustments that were part of a greater balance.

I failed, of course. Any injury or illness still wounded me. Being capable of good health is an intrinsic right we all share, but I struggled to remain apart from the pain. I worked in the commissary as part of my scholarship, doling out burgers and fries and nachos. I volunteered at one of the on-campus daycare centers as atonement, doling out band-aids and ointments and soothing words.

In the fall of my senior year I was part of my first real exhibition. The head of the art department had included two of my pieces. After much internal debate I decided to go. I had to see how I stacked up. I went anonymously, however. I didn't wear a nametag, and I didn't hover around my work like most of the other artists.

A lot of talent was represented: landscapes, still lifes, anonymous portraits, landmarks, all very good. April had taken the hood of a '56 Ford and had a nude female mannequin perched astraddle its nose, its fake breasts protruding, its hands behind its head, an afro wig dyed blue with steel wool pubic hair to match, and the whole thing chromed. It was incredible.

I had two portraits. The first depicted an ancient Hawaiian woman picking pineapple on a plantation surrounded by ridges of lava domes. I borrowed from Gauguin and had taken great pains to smooth the paint until the texture was flat to the touch. I'd also relied heavily on my tint catalogue and created patterns of color individually before applying them to canvas.

The second portrait was my mother, sitting at the piano in a summer dress, a shaft of light from the bay window illuminating her sheet music. I'd used pastel tones, again using my catalogue in a paint-by-the-numbers approach, knowing exactly where each hue would begin and end, blending them with the tips of my fingers until seamless.

My work drew attention, conversation, and close inspection. The fuss was very flattering, but I knew there was another source for their curiosity. Perhaps it was my sense of mischief or simply vanity, but I discovered hiding a pair of hands was easy.

Sometimes they were folded, as if in prayer. Sometimes they were cupped open, as a child would try to catch the rain. Sometimes they stretched outward in a pianist's flex, or the fingers slightly curved in an inaudible gasp of pain. But always two hands, and if they did not touch, they were always close together, hardly ever more than an inch or two long.

Sometimes I would forget where I'd put them and had to hunt for them myself. In the portrait of the plantation worker I'd hidden them in a stalk, nearly indistinguishable from the leaves.

In my mother's portrait they were part of the crow's feet at the corners of her eyes, nearly invisible, like the faded tracks of memory.

One buyer offered eight hundred dollars for *The Plantation* and another twelve hundred dollars for *The Piano Teacher*. I was even approached about putting more of my pieces in a catalogue. I was ecstatic and felt like a giant.

My mother was thrilled. She fussed and fawned and said that someday she was going to convert the attic into a shrine and charge admission. Her praise made me realize how much I'd missed her.

~ * ~

One night in March the phone rang. Spring break was coming soon, and I hadn't seen her since Christmas. She called at least once a week and was overdue. I smiled as I answered.

"Hello yourself," I said cheerfully.

There was a slight pause. The voice was strange, pinched, and not someone I recognized.

"Is this David O'Beirne?"

"Yes. Who's this?"

"Dr. Marvin Allen, Valley Presbyterian. I'm calling about your mother, David." He paused mid-breath. "She's had a stroke. You need to come."

My mind flashed electric white and the breath rushed from my body, and I waited for the punch line that didn't come.

"David?"

"Oh God. How bad is it?"

"The prognosis isn't favorable. The quicker you can get here, the better."

He had no way of knowing the full extent of truth in that statement, and hope rose as I forced the panic from my voice.

"You've got to do something for me."

"Anything I can."

"You've got to keep her alive until I get there. Put her on a machine if you have to, but keep her alive."

He sighed. "David, I'm afraid she won't know if you're here or not."

"God dammit, that's not the point! Either do as I ask or tell me how to transfer her to another hospital that will!"

"All right, all right. But please get here as quickly as possible."

No flights were available out of Oakland. San Francisco had a flight for LA boarding in thirty minutes. Normally, the trip to the airport would have taken twenty. I made it in fifteen, pleading with every breath, "Hang on for me, Mama. Hang on."

I remember very little of the trip, just fragments of time and dispassionate conversation of strangers doing their jobs. In less than two hours I was standing breathless at the ICU desk, feeling that there was meaning to what I had named misfortune, a greater function to all I had named misery and mercy in my antipathy.

"Dr. Allen?"

The seasoned nurse was immune to my frustration and stress. "Regarding?"

"Margaret O'Beirne."

Her eyes flickered momentarily, and she pressed a button on the phone. "Mrs. O'Beirne's son is here."

Dr. Allen was a pleasant-looking man with solid white hair. "You must be David," he said, extending his hand.

I ignored the gesture. "Where's my mother?"

The bastard actually smiled, and a sense of dread settled over me like a slow dream, then awoke like a nightmare. He turned and moved away from the desk, knowing I would follow.

"I'm so sorry, David. She didn't make it."

Blackness struck my senses, leaving only a pinprick of light to let me know I was still there, and I heard myself say feebly, "You promised."

"It wouldn't have mattered. She went into cardiac arrest, and we couldn't get her back. Why don't we go into my office."

I'd never felt such a sickening, violent rage in my life. I wanted to kill him with my bare hands. Then the music rose, the solitary note, wailing as if for a lost soul, calling to me, giving me a mere instant of clarity.

"How long?" I asked.

He looked puzzled. "An hour ago. Maybe a little less. Why don't we—"

"Where is she?"

"David..."

I had him by the neck before I knew it, and the sound coming from my throat was not me. "I said where is she?"

I could see his fear. "Downstairs. The morgue."

I ran toward the elevator and heard him call after me, "David, please..."

I moved quickly, though numbly, aware only of my movement and a single memory. I was a small child sitting in the bay window with the sun streaming in on me, the sounds of piano filling the air. I turned ever so slowly and saw her sitting there, her eyes closed as she coaxed music from beneath her fingers—

—Cold. The morgue was in a deep hallway off-limits to the public. I was aware of other people around, but no one even looked my way.

I entered. The pathologist on-duty was on the phone. He looked at me and muttered, "Thanks for the warning" at the same time. I did not panic. I was not hysterical. I simply moved to him, aware of his anxiety even as he blocked my path.

"Margaret O'Beirne," I said. "Where is she?"

"I think we should wait for Dr.—"

I had him pinned against the wall. "Now!"

He pointed to a row of lockers. "Eighteen."

I have heard that humans have no instincts. That we even have to learn to suckle. That everything is trial-and-error. I have also heard that hunters freeze when they hear the whirr of a rattlesnake, even if they haven't heard it before, knowing instinctively what the danger is.

It is the same with death. Somehow we recognize it, and do so blindly. I pulled out the drawer and knew instantly my mother was dead.

I gasped aloud and tried to still the trembling. The tears flowed freely, and I didn't care. "Oh, Mama," I whispered.

I had but one hope. I grasped both sides of her face, feeling but ignoring the cold of her flesh. I called to the music. The note came, quickly to the chord, but fitfully, like sedentary muscles unused to exercise. The chord swelled, laboriously, and I ushered it on, pushing the sound upward. I could sense the change...

...sweetness, completion. God, the relief moved me from misery to might, all within an instant. I reached deep within myself, more deeply than ever before, more deeply than I'd ever known possible, to find the infinitesimal spark I might capture to bring her back.

The music strengthened, spreading blinding light into every corner of my consciousness before flying from me. Wave after wave I gave to her. But beneath my hands was dumb flesh.

From the corner of my eye I saw the bewildered pathologist. Desperation was already beginning to mount in me.

"Come on, Mama. Come on."

Again I tried. Again everything worked perfectly. Again I managed to reach farther, absorbing the power until I could hold no more, until the swell ripped at my seams, before letting it go.

And my eyes were opened to green hills and rocky slopes bent beneath a perfect sky, a headland before a distant sea. I had no idea where I was or how I'd gotten there. At first I thought I was delirious, but she was there, standing silent against the wind, looking out over the water.

I called to her. For a moment I didn't think she'd heard. Then, slowly, she turned toward me.

Even from a distance I could see the sadness. Not the melancholy sadness of separation or loss. A sadness I'd seen before. The terrible sadness of acceptance. Then, she simply shook her head.

I would not let her go. I released all I held until it burned every corner of my consciousness as the power poured from me. Even in torment, I would not let go until I had milked every particle and given it all to her.

The image faded to the dull gray light of reality, and the sounds of voices and the awareness of arms around me. I struggled. Dr. Allen was there, and a security guard had me locked in a bear hug while another had my legs. I screamed and I was torn away, and the music vanished.

"No! No!"

~ * ~

When death is imminent all the chemicals of stored memory flood the brain with such force that there is room for nothing in consciousness but those most potent events, hurling into the mind's eye in rapid succession. I, too, was dead, but there was nothing but blackness—no memory more potent than loss.

In the distance was a vague light, a fuzzy cast that did not seem powerful enough to reveal all the secrets of the universe, but light nonetheless. I heard an indistinct sound.

"There you are."

An ungodlike face appeared in the light, and as I began to focus I realized I was lying in bed and could not move my arms or legs. My throat was dry.

"Where am I?"

"Safe," he said. "We were worried about you, and thought under the circumstances it was best to let you rest."

He seemed ancient with hardly a hair on his head. He wore a white lab coat and a stethoscope around his neck. I lay in a hospital bed, and restraining straps encased me.

"I'm Paul Samuelson," he said, unbuckling the restraints. "Sorry for this. But you were in a state when you brought you here."

I tried to gain my bearings. "How long?"

He shrugged. "Couple of days."

My head sagged back. The horror all came crashing in. My mother...

"My mother?"

"Everything's been taken care of. I believe a neighbor saw to all the details. Her wishes were very specific. The rest is waiting for you when you're up to it."

I would never be up to it. I closed my eyes, praying if there was any true benevolence in life I would be swallowed up. My mother was gone. I had failed. What was left for me?

"When can I leave?"

"In the morning. Let the medication wear off. I'd also like to arrange for you to see someone who might be able to help you on an outpatient basis. I think it would do you some good."

It couldn't possibly help, but he would never understand and I couldn't explain it. So I nodded.

He hesitated. "There's something else, David. Dr. Allen feels very badly about this. Your mother had a DNR on file. There was nothing we could do."

A voice shrieked inside my head. My voice. *Oh God, Mama! Why did you do that? Why?*

"I just want to go home," I murmured.

"Good. Just call the nurse if you need anything. You should sleep through the night."

He paused at the doorway and looked at me again. "This is none of my business..."

I knew he wouldn't leave without a response. "Yes?"

"About what... happened. What were you trying to do?"

I met his eyes and held them. I almost smiled, almost told him the truth, just to watch his reaction, just to show him how utterly little he really knew.

"I don't know." I sighed. "Just lost my head, I guess."

He held my gaze for a moment, then nodded and left.

~ * ~

I stared down at the stone. One of those practical markers set flush into the ground so the caretaker could trim around it with ease. The smooth granite bore her name and the dates. The flowers were still fresh.

Florence had driven me, crying the whole way, but had left me alone for a time. Neither of us found comfort.

I stood and stared and remembered how half a life before I had lain in my bed with the grim sounds of death all around me, and with complete and primal resolve clung to the only course remaining to me: a vain and self-indulgent denial simply because I could not cope.

Now I had killed her, my mother, my ally, my conscience.

To simply ignore the music was no longer enough. To live with my failure, to have the sound haunt my sleep, to taunt me at all waking hours, to gnaw at me daily, to erode my soul into nothingness, that was to be my destiny now.

More—it was to be my penance.

Five

In the time before I washed ashore I lived a life of avoidance. Nothing is real if it does not exist in memory, and memory can be thwarted.

I didn't have to worry about money right away. My mother was by no means wealthy, but she owned our house outright and had some savings. I sold everything except for her piano, invested it all, loaded up my old van with about forty pieces of artwork, my supplies, and a couple of boxes of personal items, and bade farewell to all I had known before.

For the first three years I explored the coast from Baja to Alaska, never in one place very long, never having a real home, building a backlog of work. It's amazing how easy it is to be anonymous. I once went several days without uttering a single word.

As much energy as I'd devoted to avoiding anyone or anything that might have claimed even the most remote attachment to me, I had learned the simplest way to foil the internal was to flood it with external good.

The landscape was truly beautiful. Mountains like misshapen hats, hills bending to promontories overlooking the Pacific, long, winding drives up the coast. Warm nights and the shadows of pines, the quiet outside the city, and NPR playing jazz in the frail hours when most of this world was sleeping. The Pacific Coast Highway had many places to take hidden walks, where I could step into the light just long enough to saturate myself, and experience the casual encounters of a nod, a smile, and moving on.

I kept returning to the Big Sur coast, the seventy-mile stretch of Highway 1 reaching from Carmel to San Simeon. The area's population swells during the long, dry summer, and I made a habit of moving inland across the Santa Lucia Mountains and the Los Padres National Forest to more remote areas.

The northernmost part of Big Sur is thick with writers, artists, and artisans who love nothing more than spending their days talking about their work, but it was great to have places where I could make a stealth run for supplies. Galleries abounded where I could have tried to sell my work if my aversion to discussing my art had been a hundred times weaker and my confidence in it a hundred times stronger.

Early in the fourth year I needed to make a supply run, but it was snowing heavily and parts of the highway were closed. Southeast of Lucia, between Highway 1 and Highway 101, I came to a town with a small art gallery. The entire town seemed empty, but there were lights on in the gallery and I parked.

A bell sounded as I entered, followed almost immediately by a brassy voice. "I'll be right with you." I saw her across the way, discussing a piece with a customer.

The quality and variety of the work surprised me. Seascapes with escarpments, mountain and forest scenes brought local flavor, but she also had nameless portraits, desert vistas, and universal still lifes.

I didn't see a supply section, so I decided to move on. On my way out something through a cracked door caught my eye and held me. I moved transfixed toward a small office. On the wall was the portrait of a young man and a small boy. The young man was actually Maggie, juxtaposed in a Naval uniform, and the boy was me. The painting was one of the two pieces I had submitted for the catalogue after my first exhibition during my senior year. Strangely, I wanted to touch it, to feel the living canvas beneath my fingers once again, to embrace it and reclaim it.

Beneath the painting was a small gold plaque that read *Fatherless Child*. I never really named my work.

"It's not for sale," she said.

I turned. She was in her sixties, barely over five feet tall with a steel-gray pageboy and an unmistakable New York voice softened but not erased by distance and time.

"I paid fifteen hundred dollars for it a few years back. Know what it's worth now? Five times that."

I was flattered. "Really."

"Some kid from Berkeley did it."

"Why is it called *Fatherless Child?*"

"I did that. Any idiot can tell it's a woman's face. Wish I had ten more like it. So what can I do for you?"

Shifting my attention was difficult. "I was actually looking for supplies. Guess I'll just wait."

"You an artist?"

I shrugged.

"You're cleaner than most."

I grinned. "I know how to use a razor."

I moved toward the door. She followed part of the way. I paused. Asking was foolish, I knew, but I couldn't seem to help myself. "If you had ten more, what do you think you could sell them for?"

"Pardon?"

"Paintings like the one in your office. What could you sell them for?"

She eyed me warily for a moment. "One twenty-five, a hundred fifty thousand, maybe."

"I thought you said that one was worth seventy-five hundred."

She took a step closer. "Well you wouldn't just throw them out there. You'd do a couple at a time, see, over two or three years. Bring the price up piece-by-piece."

"Oh," I said. "Just curious. Thanks."

She followed me a few steps and spoke to my back. "There's a patch on the uniform that shows his rank. You know what's hidden in there?"

I stopped. It didn't really matter now. I turned and looked at her.

"Hands," I said.

"Oh my God."

~ * ~

We were driving west toward the coast, skirting the edge of the forest. Big Sur is rugged, mountainous terrain, where the peaks drop precipitously toward the sea. The whole area is surprisingly rural. Most of the practical development has already been done, many plots have scenic easements or deed restrictions, and various governments own the rest.

We turned down a dirt road lined with Santa Lucia fir near a stand of coast redwoods. After a couple of hundred yards we stopped.

The house stood on a small, oblong lot. The land had been cleared except for a large live oak tree standing watch over the cliff, but it was sheltered by woods in all directions. Patches of seacliff buckwheat and outcroppings led to the ocean a hundred feet below, where I could see jade coves and large offshore rocks. The house wasn't much more than a cabin, but I stared entranced. I'd never grown tired of the views.

"Jeanette Hargrave is an old friend of mine," she said. "Her husband died last year, and both her daughters have settled back east."

I kept watch. I could see a couple of pleasure boats in the distance. "It's incredible."

"She wants to be in the same time zone as her grandchildren. She wants to sell, but she doesn't want some developer's hands on it, sticking a couple of duplexes out here. It's private. Nearest neighbor is over a half mile away."

I looked at her. "I can't afford anything like this."

She scowled. "You've been living in that glorified motel for what, two years now? And I sell your work, remember. Besides, you were loaded when you got here."

"That's my mother's."

She smiled gently. "I meant no disrespect. All I'm saying is that if you want it, I know we can work it out."

I looked outward again to over two hundred feet of broken shoreline north and south. The property was perfect, and perfection has the complete luxury of impatience.

I smiled in her direction. "I want it."

~ * ~

We stuck to Mrs. Felker's plan, and issued about six pieces a year. She handled all the details and acted as my agent. She has a great reputation, but will still shamelessly sell coastline prints of sea lions to tourists at the drop of a hat. Over the last couple of years my pieces sold for an average of twenty-five to fifty thousand dollars each. I added space in every direction, gutted the house, and put back as few walls as possible. I built a large deck in the back and adopted it as my bay window, where on clear days I watch the Pacific.

I devoted a room to over a dozen flat architectural file cabinets, each drawer containing as many as five carefully wrapped pieces; the total inventory was about three hundred. Many were rejects, but I had about a hundred pieces that didn't make me cringe.

I was still prolific and often worked in the dead-of-night, and in the same mesmeric trance where I was hardly aware of anything, just as I had done since my youth, and for the same reason.

The music was still there, from the note and its company to the chord, and to its eventual movement that only comes in my sleep when I am helpless to push it back. But I never consciously acknowledged the power. And I never yielded.

Mrs. Felker still liked to name my pieces. I still couldn't care less. Last month she sold *Mother and Child* for a hundred thousand dollars. The painting was reviewed in *ARTnews Magazine*, and because the color separations for the accompanying photograph tended to accentuate the darker tones, there woven into the mother's hair was an unintentionally conspicuous pair of open hands clasped at the thumbs like the shadow puppet of a bird.

Soon, anyone with access to the other forty or so pieces in circulation searched for and found the hands. Those hands made me a commodity, God forbid.

It had been ten years since my mother died. Of my life before, I had her piano in the center of my large, open front room. And buried somewhere in the recesses of my files was the crude portrait of a forlorn boy with no hands.

I was thirty-two years old, nearly self-sufficient and perhaps nearly as much alone. I still avoided personal attention but made a deliberate effort every day to appreciate my good fortune. I relished my work and the security it brought, and I loved the sanctuary of my home.

At the moment I was working on a panorama of about a quarter-mile of cliffs, which was something new for me and difficult. The piece was about forty inches tall and nearly eighty inches wide, and the amount of detail was formidable. I finally got an acceptable background, but I was struggling with the faces of a couple of sea otters. Minutia, to be sure, but the first effort made them look like Disney characters and the second like creatures from a low-budget horror flick, so I was left to wonder if I could find an acceptable compromise or should just quit.

My phone rang. I stopped and wiped my hands. It rang four, five, six times. Only a handful of people even had my number. Eight, nine, ten. The woman had boundless patience.

"Hello?"

"You're the only person on this planet without voicemail," she said. She has a voice like soft Brillo.

"No," I teased.

"No, what?"

"No to whatever it is you want me to do but already know I don't want to do it."

She sighed. "Even if it's for your own good?"

"Especially if it's for my own good."

"Why not?"

I laughed. "Good Lord, Mrs. Felker, I don't even know what you want."

I could hear her smile through the phone. "You have this awful knack..."

"I know. And I'm sorry. So what's up?"

"You know I've been working with that old fart Drexel in San Francisco."

Arthur Drexel is one of the most reputable art dealers and auctioneers in the world, and he's probably younger than she is. People lobby just to be put on his invitation list.

"Yes."

"Trust me, the man's an egocentric pain in the ass who wouldn't know a decent piece of art if it jumped down his shorts, but he does have contacts."

So the news wasn't good. Maybe Disney wasn't such a bad idea after all.

"He wants to do an entire collection. A dozen pieces."

Heat rose in my face, and pricklies erupted on the back of my neck.

"This could mean a lot of money," she continued. "Over a million, certainly."

"Ain't life grand?" I said numbly.

"Yes, it is."

"What's the catch?"

"Always so sanguine, my dear ray of sunshine."

"You're saying there isn't one?"

"He wants you there," she said simply. "I needn't remind you that these aren't going to be tourists from Ohio. These are real collectors who like to spend money."

"I wouldn't feel comfortable being there with the bidding going on."

"We're talking before. Or after. Just to mingle a little."

I hated the idea. "Well, I'm right in the middle—"

"—Of a very crucial stage. Yes, I know. Your work requires your complete attention. It wouldn't hurt you to get out. See what's going on in the world."

"I know what's going on in the world. I've got a satellite dish."

"Well, think about it. Normally I would say by being there you could charm another quarter million out of the deal, but you don't care about money either. So when can I look at the pieces?"

Suddenly, I felt cheery. "Tomorrow. Come for lunch."

"Good. And do think about going. *Mother and Child* really shook things up. People are curious."

"What if I don't want to be a curiosity?"

"You're just going to have to accept that you're on the verge of becoming a very famous man."

"Well, I always wanted to be famous," I said.

"No, just notorious enough to drive little old ladies crazy."

"You're not that little."

"Old joke, David."

"So it is."

"No Mexican for lunch, okay? My system won't take it."

"*Hasta manana.*"

~ * ~

I tried to work but couldn't. Elation was such a rare companion. I could never have envisioned my work would lead me to this point.

I moved outside. The sky was clear and the season was that time between spring and summer when the warmth was like a light wrap. I recognized the moment. These were tenuous, these ascendant times that could not be summoned or manipulated, only relished at their dawning.

I closed my eyes and saw the pink light through my eyelids.

"God, I do love it here," I whispered.

A public beach lay about a mile south of me. I had to walk overland about half way before descending, but I decided to go the distance. I knew the beach wouldn't be very crowded this time in May.

Strong currents, waves, and frigid waters made swimming hazardous, but those conditions didn't discourage the hearty and foolhardy. During July there would be as many as a thousand people on this stretch of sand. Now there were perhaps fifteen, mostly immobile fishermen stretched a couple hundred yards apart, looking as much a part of the natural scape as the rocks and driftwood. I had done a portrait of an ancient fisherman a couple of years ago, and the Key West Chamber of Commerce bought it.

Gypsy vendors would hawk soda and ice cream from Memorial Day to Labor Day in a row of little white igloos, eighteen hours a day, before moving on. Anything was possible during the summer. It was going to be a good year.

I eschewed the walkway and moved along the waterline. A few sunbathers and a couple of mothers letting their children run themselves weary were the only people on the sand, and in the distance a pair of college-aged kids enjoying their early parole tossed a Frisbee.

I put on my sunglasses, feeling invisible. A fishing trawler moved north nearly a mile offshore. I could still hear the echo of its engine. I continued to look westward until the sea and sky merged and I could not distinguish between them.

We were not born of earth. We were born of water. And the gods of grace and fickle events did not fall from the sky. They rose in wisps and fog from the sea. Whatever else we are, our oldest stored recollection is of a life submerged in breaths of primordial and liquid air.

I was lonely. I thrived in solitude but loneliness isn't solitude. Loneliness is the unwilling collaboration with and surrender to the awful arbitrariness of life, a collusion with the Fates to survive with no greater expectation.

I was just about to turn back when I heard a shrill cry. A woman's voice, piercing the distance in its pain. I strained to look and didn't see the source at first. I found her on the second pass. The two college kids were dragging a man from the water, an older man by the look of it, bald head and round gray belly. His wife ran to the water's edge, her hands outstretched, her siren wail floating atop the pounding surf.

The music came unbidden, along with the intimate knot in the pit of my stomach. The note called to me just as it called to its ilk. I hesitated and looked back over my shoulder toward escape. Slipping away unknown would be easy.

I began a quick walk toward them. The kids seemed to know what they were doing. One began CPR and the other began mouth-to-mouth, the woman looming in grating distraction. They stopped for a moment. The kid doing mouth-to-mouth pressed an ear to the man's chest. I could see him shake his head.

The notes fluttered, and I sped up. They were doing it wrong. His hands were pressing too far toward the center. *No*, I said to myself. *Left of the sternum.*

The chord came, and I moved to a trot, or rather my legs moved in spite of me. The chord grew louder, waiting for me, prodding me, chastising me for such protracted neglect, roaring inside my head. I hated this. I hated the fear. I hated being defenseless against it. I hated knowing what I could not unknow.

The chord swelled, urging me to its bidding, just as the scene before me changed. The movement upon the man's chest was frantic, the other blowing in desperate equal measure. They were failing, and the man's wife cried louder.

I ran at a full sprint, prepared to let the music go. I could feign CPR and hope for the best. My fingers began to flex unconsciously. The chord grew louder, a crescendo toward the unknown. I tried to keep it apart from me, apart from the life I had worked so hard to build.

Yet the song began to draw me in. I was a child again held captive by its sweetness, an accomplice to its will. I felt the power encase me as the outside world began to fade. Then, the blighted recollections—I was a young boy again, impotent, handless, weeping...

Suddenly the man coughed, water spurting as he forced life into his lungs. The boys shouted and exchanged high fives, then rolled him onto his side until his breathing normalized. His wife moved to him, the onlookers cheered, and an ambulance pulled up to the curb near the walkway.

Still outside the ring, I slowed to a walk. I was part of the world again, of warm wind and salty air. All surroundings returned to being, and I stood there unseen and unnoticed, and the music grudgingly began to subside.

To my surprise I realized I'd been crying, and I wiped my cheeks with my thumbs. Yet I welcomed the validity of it all, that there was justice and purity in my aloneness, my exile.

I turned on my heels and went home. I put on the headphones and listened to Mahler's *Songs of a Wayfarer* as loud as I could stand.

Six

Sara Rembert packed. Encasing all her belongings was a simple thing, and that bothered her. Three suitcases, a trunk, a couple of hanging bags, and several boxes held everything she owned.

She owed the state five years for her scholarship, but she would start with no debt, forty-five hundred dollars in savings, her wits, her will, and a car long past redemption.

Work was everything to her. Third in her class at UCLA. Sixth in its medical school. One of only four accepted into the trauma program at Christ's in San Francisco. One of only two to complete the program. A decade of constant study and work.

So when all her options to satisfy her scholarship requirements had been presented, she had taken the smallest, the least prestigious. She knew why. The chance to prove herself, to be absolutely necessary.

Her best friend, Marty, was an ad exec she'd treated for a concussion sustained while rollerblading. They sat together at Dempsey's near the wharf, having the last of their weekly lunch-and-gab sessions.

Marty had said their friendship worked because they were too toxic for anyone else and weren't in competition with each other, but they would miss each other terribly.

Sara was weary of competition, the almost imposed need to be the best, to prevail. All she wanted now was to work. All she wanted now was peace.

She stared at a holographic spot in the general direction of Oakland, idly stirring her coffee. Marty looked up from her fruit salad with a grin.

"You know, if you were really sure you'd made the right choice you wouldn't be second-guessing yourself."

Sara switched gears in mid-air, looking at Marty intently, a trick, now a habit, she'd learned her first year of residency to gain a patient's confidence.

"What makes you think I'm second-guessing myself?"

"You're stirring black coffee. And don't give me that Doctor Sara look. I'm very much intact, thank you."

Sara smiled and put down her spoon. "You certainly are."

"So what's the problem?"

She shook her head. "Ocean Park. The cusp of the universe. God, I hope I don't fall on my ass."

"Please. Those people have probably never even heard of anesthesia before."

Sara stabbed at a chunk of potato in her soup and left it stuck on her fork. "I want to be where I can do some good."

"You could do that anywhere."

"This place was just a clinic a few years ago, and there's like a billion people there during the summer. They've always had to ship out trauma patients. Sometimes twenty minutes is too long. I can help. They bought some good equipment."

"And now they've bought you."

"Rented me." She paused. "And, it's very pretty there. Besides, it's less than two hundred miles from here."

"True. So what about..."
"What?"
Marty smirked and shrugged.
"What?" Sara repeated.
"Homo Erectus?"
"What are you talking about?"
"Menfolk, Sara. Lock and load. You know. Boys."
She shook her head. "Who cares about that?"
"You don't?"

She thought for a moment. She hadn't dated in so long she wasn't sure she remembered how to care about such things. "No. I really don't."

"Me, either," Marty said.

They exchanged long looks and then began to laugh.

"All the locals are probably ancient anyway," Sara said.

"Harder to train, easier to manage," Marty retorted.

~ * ~

Dr. Charles Evans was the director of operations at Mid Coastal. A genuinely warm man who still loved his work after nearly thirty-five years, he had been a founder of the clinic that had become the hospital, and the man most instrumental in convincing her to come.

Sara was hanging her credentials and awards on the wall of her cramped office when there was a knock on the door and he stuck his head in.

"Settling in?"
"Yes. Come in."
"Sorry about the space. We thought the new ER should take priority."
"It's fine."
"We'll get your name on the door tomorrow."
"You might want to wait a couple of weeks."

He waved off her modesty. "It should be obvious we need you desperately. The whole staff is very excited about it." He sat on the edge of the desk and looked at her seriously. "Big Sur has a hospital less than a half hour away by ambulance. We have Air Evac to San Francisco. But on my desk is a box with sixteen files in it. Sixteen people I honestly believe we could've saved last year if we'd had someone here. I look at it every day."

"I'll get my feet wet soon, and then we'll know."

"Oh, I already know. And you may not be able to get your feet wet. You may have to jump in at high tide."

Sara grinned. "I'm a good swimmer."

"Yes. I'll just bet you are."

~ * ~

I enjoyed experimenting with food, and getting my hands into something solid felt good. I made a cold salad from lobster boiled in beer and a mustard coleslaw I'd seen on The Food Network at three o'clock in the morning. I had club soda with lime and a chocolate chip cheesecake I'd made from scratch. Maybe I should've been a chef.

I had pulled twenty pieces for Mrs. Felker to see. I didn't want her snooping around my lair even though she might've made better choices. I was never completely comfortable about any of my work, so if I was relatively satisfied with the twenty, I knew she could pick a dozen from them.

She was early. She was always early. I had heard she would get busy and keep people waiting for forty-five minutes, but she was never late to one of our meetings. Punctuality was one of the ways she looked out for me.

We chatted during lunch, and she spent most of the time trying to shame me into going. I'd already decided to go but didn't want to spoil her fun.

Afterward we moved into the living room. I had a loveseat perfect for napping, and she sat. She took the reading glasses she wore on a chain around her neck and stuck them on the end of her nose. I had neatly placed the canvases within reach.

She took the first. "Still trying to keep me out of the studio, I see."

"Nothing personal," I answered.

She studied the painting. Even after all this time, watching her examine my work still made me uneasy. I should have been doing something else.

"I'm not dense, you know. I know you're holding out on me."

I didn't respond.

Flattery wasn't her style, which I appreciated, but she was always so focused I could never tell what was going on inside her head.

In my opinion the best of the group was a large panorama of the sea at night, with a storm brewing on the horizon. Getting the detail right had taken me months, and I had experimented with every color imaginable to get the proper illumination behind the range of black and gray.

After three pieces she made her first comment. "Excellent, as usual. Very good stuff, David. I wanted to get away from sea themes a bit for this collection. Let everyone know you're not just about California. Except *Night Sky*, of course."

"How about *Dogs Playing Poker*?"

"I'll ignore that."

"Why do you always want to name everything?"

A title gives them an identity people can hold onto."

She smiled broadly at the next one and put it on the easel. She handled the painting so lovingly I felt her pleasure. "*The Teacher.*"

The portrait was a little girl at a piano, studious in that juvenile way while her teacher bent near to rearrange her fingers.

"You've used that already," I said.

She ignored me. "Doesn't resemble her as much as some of the others."

I knew she meant my mother. We'd known each other too long for me to deny it. "Younger version."

"And the girl?"

Sheila Adams. "No one in particular."

She looked at me over her glasses in a way that made me feel I was in grade school again. "So, where are they?"

I cracked a smile. "Where are what?"

It took her nearly a minute, but she found them, this time clasped tightly together as if in a child's fervent prayer, blended into the dark wood of the music stand atop the piano.

"Exquisite, David. Simply addictive."

"Ka-ching."

She knew me too well to be hurt, and she remained engrossed in the work. "All this background. You'd miss it if it wasn't there, but it meshes so perfectly. The clock, the wallpaper, the banister. Her concentration is so intense. Her barrette is shaped like a bicycle. What does that mean?"

"Nothing specific."

"Well, your detail is getting better and better."

We disagreed only on the last. I had done a still life several years before of an old fishing boat, obsolete and in decay, lying akilter in high grass, abandoned and forgotten. The hands were almost invisible, hidden in the faded name upon its bow—*The Cubit*. I had tried to give it a faded, washed look and had never been satisfied with the result.

"It's too raw," I said.

"I like it," she said. "Besides, it will be a good opener. Drive up the bidding on the rest of the collection."

"The love of money is the root of all evil," I said.

Her smile was almost sinister. "Ain't that a bitch."

~ * ~

Crowds are very troublesome for me. Sometimes when I am thrust into the midst of hundreds of people moving about, however unacknowledged, I can feel their collective pain. I can move down a congested sidewalk and sense an incoherent mass of aches and ills, the blur of so many separate deficiencies.

On these occasions I have to maintain such great effort to force the music back that I am always exhausted afterward, and later the music invariably invades my sleep to blare its displeasure at my denial until I often have to take a pill and wear a dark mask just to rest a bit.

Still, San Francisco is bewitching, and from the first moment its wonder slowly seeps into my senses, and I am engulfed in unexpected pleasure. The city is a twenty-first-century Rome with the same seven hills, the same architectural excesses, the same interior dramas, and the same debauchery. Everything on earth exists somewhere in San Francisco, and only there can you find so much literature among its ruins and so much putrescence in its gilded towers.

More, it is matchless, and I let it take me.

Mrs. Felker had put me in the Mark Hopkins, a nice touch, and I loved the view of the city from Nob Hill. But I wanted to forego Union Square and Chinatown, and instead spent much of the afternoon near the old Haight-Ashbury. Hip-hop blasting from boom boxes had replaced the distant vestiges of psychedelic colors and smoke-filled air, but I ambled into Buena Vista Park and found a sunny place to sit where it was relatively quiet.

Even so, I saw a couple of kids smoking a joint, a Marine with a buzz cut walking a standard poodle, two black women at least eighty holding hands, and an old Asian man with a gray Ho Chi Minh goatee skateboarding.

The world of ordinary drama is an exhilarating place.

~ * ~

Drexel's loft was on Powell St. near Fisherman's Wharf in an old warehouse converted into downstairs and upstairs showrooms. The studio was all oak floors, painted steel beams, and whitewashed walls, and he was a master of display.

A sign near the elevator announced the auction with *By Invitation Only* in small print at the bottom.

Upstairs, each piece was partitioned off, lit separately, and seemed to be in random order, except as I moved among them I found a sense of continuity with the last pieces to be auctioned nearest the makeshift dais.

Fewer than fifty people were in attendance, mostly dealers and collectors with enormous experience, and a few representing houses and collectors unknown even to Drexel himself. A color catalogue had been produced in advance, and people milled about, studying pieces or going from a catalogue picture to the accompanying piece and back.

I thumbed through a catalogue while a lady with pink hair greeted people as they entered. I managed to sneak in unnoticed behind a couple. No one wore badges anyway.

I didn't see Mrs. Felker and was ignored on the whole. I tried to assay reaction as much as I could, but no one gave the slightest indication as to what they really thought, as if all life was poker where money and the upper hand were involved. The experience was all very complimentary and all very unnerving.

If I found Mrs. Felker I'd find Drexel, and I wanted to offer my profound gratitude and humility before getting the hell out of there. I saw them near the dais and began to wend my way toward them.

As I approached, a man standing in front of *The Teacher* caught my eye. He looked even more out of place than I did. He didn't look like a collector. He looked like a roadie for the Beach Boys. He had long gray hair pulled into a ponytail, a full beard, and sunglasses. He wore a blue Hawaiian shirt with white jeans and old-fashioned deck shoes without logos or exotica. And he pored over the image without moving, as if he were a performance artist and he and the painting were a part of the same piece.

Mrs. Felker saw me and approached. "Almost time for one of your phantom escapes," she whispered. "Just shake the old fart's hand and we'll call it even."

"Who is that?" I whispered in return.

"Jack Baird." She smiled. "I asked Drexel the same thing. Made a fortune refurbishing old motels along the coast or some such." Then she pulled me away.

~ * ~

I couldn't relax in the hotel room. I was restless and shaky. The anxiety wasn't the music. My fit of nerves was something else. Part of the problem was being out of my element, and part of it was knowing that people were haggling over something that was so hard for me to let go, and I was so disconnected from the process.

I took the Powell-Hyde Line all the way down to the Hyde Street Pier and the waterfront. You could still see Alcatraz and the old lighthouse. A cruise ship was moving out into the bay. The same body of water I stared at from my back door, but I still felt isolated and apart from it. The view was glorious, but it was beyond my grasp. I wanted to go home.

A note awaited when I returned. Mrs. Felker had scribbled it on hotel stationery and left it on my pillow.

Two point one million, my love. Night Sky *brought two-twenty. Jack Baird paid two-forty for* The Teacher.

Seven

Highway One is still only two lanes, serpentine and slow, and death to anyone who wanders too close to the edge. Even so, I loved to drive it, especially at night when traffic was light and salt-smell permeated the air.

NPR was featuring a live recording of Charlie Parker from some long-forgotten European gig. It was past two a.m. when I cut across to 101 about twenty miles north of home.

My life had changed again. I was the embodiment of unforeseen good, the beneficiary of some rare karmic delight. Whatever lay ahead, I could not deny the moment, nor would I be ungrateful for it. I was alive.

I'd begun to pass the outskirts of Ocean Park, a new apartment complex, and a strip shopping center, when I saw the little car. An old VW Beetle was struggling up the next hill. It was losing power, its taillights flickering and its engine popping and shooting sharp puffs of smoke out a tailpipe.

The poor beast wouldn't make it up the hill, and I watched it coast off the road. The highway had only a narrow shoulder, and the car was in a precarious position. Truckers still used the highway and needed every inch of asphalt.

I didn't want to stop. Probably kids out past curfew or a folkie moving from one gig to another. I was still clicking off the reasons inside my head when I pulled in behind the bug. I grabbed my flashlight and got out.

The first thing I heard was a loud "Shit!" The driver tried to start the engine again, but it just groaned.

I made a wide circle toward the front. The last thing I wanted was a startled motorist shooting me. I shined my flashlight across the hood to illuminate the area without hitting the driver in the face. A woman. I smiled harmlessly.

"Need some help?"

She was about my age. Her hair was short and perfectly straight. She wore very little makeup, but her skin was unblemished. She stuck her face out the window a little.

"Know anything about antiques?"

"I know you've probably got a bad alternator, a bad battery, bad cables, or any combination of the above. Or the car's just getting even for such a slow and agonizing death."

She smiled, short and controlled, sweet like a single bite of ice cream. "My mother taught me to never accept rides from strangers."

"I can call someone."

"No one to call," she said. She got out of her car and stuck out her hand. She was tall, not even a head shorter than I was. "Sara Rembert."

I shook her hand. "David O'Beirne."

She locked her car and walked back to my Jeep. I still kept my distance, letting her open her door and climb in before I opened mine. I handed her the flashlight to make her feel more secure. I left the interior light on even as we pulled away. I couldn't be sure, but I think she grinned out her window.

"Where to?"

"The Cove. You know it?"

I nodded. The Cove had upscale apartments and townhomes and a nice view of the river. "You can turn the light off," she said.

I did, but we rode in silence. The hush suited me. After a few moments she spoke. "Thanks for the lift. Probably would've had to walk. You live around here?"

"Yeah. Just getting home from a business trip to San Francisco."

"Really? I just moved here from there."

"You must've been desperate. And I hope you like sedate."

"New job. But I do like sedate."

I found myself enjoying the company, her light fragrance and husky voice. "What are you doing out this time of night?" I asked.

"Actually, I was going in to work awhile."

"You keep worse hours than I do."

"I get a lot done when it's quiet."

"Yeah, me, too."

We were interrupted by her pager. The beeping took me by surprise, but concern marked her face.

"I really hate to impose, David, but could you take me to MCM? I have an emergency."

"The hospital? Sure. Not family, I hope."

"I'm a doctor," she said. "I'm on call."

~ * ~

An otherwise sound human body violated by injury is so unnatural, beyond the obvious, that it creates its own chaos. The combination of shock and disbelief and pain breeds such irrationality. Some part of ourselves has been so carelessly torn that we retreat to the elemental, howling mindlessly and flailing at the air.

Sara had seen this reaction many times and was prepared for it. This time was no different, except this particular body weighed nearly three hundred pounds and was still fighting the paramedics as they wheeled him in.

His face was locked in a pasty blue grimace, and both hands sought purchase in loose shirts, slapped away only to return in some bizarre ritual. Below his knee were the telltale signs of a compound fracture: bone protruding through muscle and tissue, blood steadily gushing.

She immediately went to the leg, cutting away shredded jeans. The biker swatted at her.

"Hey! Back the hell off!"

She made eye contact without levity. "I'm all you've got, pal, so just take it easy and we'll get through this okay."

As she bent down again the man grabbed a handful of hair just below her crown. The paramedics jumped to pry his hand loose. But Sara was quicker. She reached back with her thumb and jabbed it hard into the joint between his second and third knuckle. His fingers opened involuntarily. Then she pressed her hand firmly in the middle of his chest and pushed him back down.

"That does it," she said calmly. "Let's just amputate it here."

And that's when he lost consciousness.

~ * ~

Five hours later she was still there, still making rounds and reviewing charts. A full house tonight, and it was only May. It was nearly dawn, and she stretched to find relief, finding little. Her shoulders were tight knots and her legs felt like rubber.

She stole into Mr. Sims' room. She'd learned a long time ago to move at nearly full-speed and make no sound—the Zen of motion. Once a fellow intern had told her she would have made a great assassin.

Even so, the big man stirred. "Hey, Doc," he mumbled, still sedated, still enjoying the drugs.

"Sorry I woke you," she said, face-down in his chart.

"You didn't. Getting hungry."

"Breakfast will be soon."

He made a face. "Any way I can get a pizza? Maybe some wings?" The upper part of his mouth looked like a goalpost when he smiled.

"Can't help you there."

She checked his IV and started for the door.

"Hey, Doc?"

She turned.

"Sorry about grabbin' you like that."

"Your leg is broken in four places. I would expect a little crankiness."

"Will it be okay?"

"In time, it will be perfect."

He nodded and pulled the thin blanket up under his chin. "Thanks," he said, yawning. Then he was gone again.

Sara smiled to herself. "You're welcome."

~ * ~

Despite my neuroses, or perhaps because of them, I consider myself enlightened, avoiding prejudice of every sort, judging no one on any form of social criteria, leaving every spare soul free to pursue his own purposes without my opinion or intrusion.

I have three exceptions, and in my own defense I do this for my own preservation, and because of secrets I alone harbor and I alone understand.

The first is any member of the press. I watch the news, tolerate some commentary, but never deceive myself as to what would happen should all the substances of my life be exposed.

The second and third are a little more subjective, and perhaps even somewhat narrow-minded on my part, certainly not a source of pride for me, and more difficult to defend: ministers and doctors.

I do not pretend to understand God. I am not at all certain there is any higher power at work in me. A force resides in me I did not ask for and do not want, an irreconcilable aptitude, but I certainly do not blame God for it. Neither do I conceive it as a gift or bounty. It simply is, and I am reluctant to attribute such a power to God at all, as good or ill, and am equally reluctant to have it interpreted by anyone, especially any self-described spiritual aspirant who has not had firsthand experience living with it and its consequences.

I simply do not trust doctors. I have been to doctors, grateful for their treatment, but am always aware that should we ever move beyond the most superficial encounters I would be at risk.

First could be an explanation of some unusual brain chemistry, or remarkable neuron activity, but the inevitable result would have me being probed and prodded and exposed with no more conscience than if I was a cadaver.

I accept ministers and doctors as representatives of the spiritual nature and the scientific nature, and I leave them both to those pursuits each earnestly believes better serves the world. But one of the liberties each of the six-plus billion of us share is the right to identify and avoid a threat.

Still, I wish that fact was not so and bear no ill will.

Now, I sit. I sit because I don't know what to do with myself. Mrs. Felker mailed me a check for nearly a million-two with the explanation she and Drexel split the twenty per-cent fee and she made tax deposits for me because she knew I'd forget. I have nearly two million dollars with a guy in LA, should never have to worry about money again, and still don't know what to do with myself.

Every artist has his own process. Even if he doesn't have a process, that's a process. Sometimes I have a sudden burst of inspiration and my hands move faster than I can think. I can always go back and renovate once I have the basic images in place.

Sometimes I doodle. I'll sit and think, my chin resting in the palm of my hand, and doodle while thinking. Sometimes the doodling doesn't have anything to do with what I'm thinking about. Sometimes the scribbling has more value, and I'll awaken to something and drop everything else to capture the image.

I was sitting and thinking and doodling. I looked down. The lines on my pad joined at the bottom into a narrow U. They moved upward and outward, and other lines framed the U in short, straight hair. Thin eyebrows, narrow-set eyes, sharp nose, high cheekbones, a tight mouth with a trace of smile, a face... her face.

I pushed the sketch aside and started to wad it up. I couldn't. I turned the drawing upside down and covered it with the pad so at least I wouldn't have to look at it. It was very late so I went to bed. I picked up a book I'd been reading about the simultaneous occupation of ancient Europe by both Cro-Magnon and Neanderthal Man. I read four or five pages before I realized I couldn't remember a damn thing I'd just read.

This was ludicrous. I had only one way to put this to rest. I looked up the number. I knew she wouldn't be there, and then at least I could sleep. I punched in the numbers. The phone rang.

"Mid Coastal Medical."

"Yes, is Dr. Rembert there, please?" I sounded like a telemarketer.

Silence. Ten seconds later she answered, and I had no idea what to say.

"Dr. Rembert."

"Sara? David O'Beirne. I don't know if you remember me or not."

"Of course. My rescuer."

"It was on my way."

She laughed, but I felt like an ass.

"I suppose you know that it's four in the morning," she said.

"Yeah, well I work pretty weird hours sometimes."

"Me, too. Obviously. So what can I do for you?"

"Well, I know you're new here. Just wanted to see if you'd like to go to breakfast."

"Sure. Can you pick me up here?"

I thought she'd be busy or at the very least, too tired. Now what? "Uh, sure. When?"

"Five-thirty?"

"I'll be there."

"I'll be waiting."

And it was just that simple. What the hell had I done?

~ * ~

A BP truck stop south of town on 101 served breakfast twenty-four hours a day and provided a modicum of privacy for people who wanted booths. Everyone minded his own business, and except for the roar of diesel engines coming and going, the restaurant was quiet.

She sat across from me, her eyes twinkling from lack of sleep. This was the first time I'd seen her in decent lighting, and she looked fabulous, the most noticeable difference between my mental image and reality being a slight gap in her two front teeth.

She took in a deep breath. "Smell that cholesterol."

"I think that's diesel fuel."

She buried her face in a yellowed menu. "Same thing."

The waitress came and we ordered. Scrambled eggs all around with toast and real butter, strawberry preserves in those little square containers, and coffee strong enough to melt lead.

She talked and ate at the same time. I loved it. "So. You a native?"

"No. I took a little break after school and found this place by accident. I liked it. Seemed serene."

"And sedate."

"At least."

"So why serenity. Why not noise?"

"Too noisy."

"Ah."

"What about you?"

She mimicked my shrug. "I owe the illustrious State of California five years of service for paying my way through med school. This was on the short list of options. I'm still surprised."

"Surprised it was on the list?"

"Surprised they wanted me."

"Why? Don't you know what you're doing?"

"Oh, I know what I'm doing. But I'm still a rookie... with a limited track record... female."

"I didn't think that made a difference anymore."

"Would you let me operate on you?"

"No."

"There you have it."

"I wouldn't let anyone operate on me."

"Even if you needed it?"

I shook my head. "Allergic to stainless steel."

"Yeah, I know what you mean. At least it's not personal."

I smiled a little. "Never that."

She fell silent, and a weariness in her face seemed much older than a single shift would account for. I thought I understood. She had more responsibility than she'd ever bargained for. The spark quickly returned.

"I am good at what I do."

"I'm sure."

"Are you?"

"Still trying to figure that one out."

"Which is?"

I grinned. "Another story. Another time."

"I'd like that," she said.

"What?"

"Another time." She forked eggs into her mouth with a look that was near deadly.

"So would I," I answered.

Eight

One of the ironies of the dichotomous existence, the state where one's well-being is almost solely determined by the periodic ebb and flow of external forces, is that sooner or later a spontaneous time of contentment will arrive unsolicited, and must be confirmed and held tightly, no matter how confounding, before the psychic weather changes, or else be lost.

I was completely and utterly directionless, but smiling so much felt good.

"You're famous," she said.

I hadn't spoken to her since the breakfast. My first thought was to wonder how she'd gotten my number, my second, that I was flattered she'd gone to the trouble.

"A rumor," I answered. "A salacious rumor."

"Well, do you know Charles Evans?"

"No."

"He's my boss. He and his wife have been helping me along, showing me around to get my bearings."

"We're a wealth of social consciousness here."

"Took me to a gallery in town. Introduced me to a lady named Felker."

"She's no lady."

"So, you're famous."

"Only to a handful who have too much free time."

"Rich, too, from what I understand."

"Good God. Did she tell you that?"

I heard that liquid laugh of hers. "She gave me your number. I hope you don't mind."

"No, of course not. I'm glad you called."

"She seemed to think it was a good idea."

"I'll bet she did. What else did she tell you?"

"That you're an enigma."

"She only does that because she's mercenary. It helps her sell my stuff."

"She loves you," she said.

I thought it was an odd thing to say. No clarification, no explanation, no embellishment, just *she loves you* as a simple statement of fact. Then I heard a buzzer in the background, and knew she was being paged.

"Gotta run," she said quickly. "Call me, okay?"

"Soon," I said.

"David?"

"Yeah?"

"You are really good at what you do."

"Thanks," I said, and hung up.

~ * ~

I stood in the sand near the water's edge at the time of day when the oncoming dusk creates a cascade of tiny lights on the waves, and in that glitter, mirage was indistinguishable from matter.

She rose from its gleaming center as if emerging from the water itself, though when she stood free she was not wet.

She wore a white dress, cut plain like a frock, smiling at me wisely, as if she already knew every hidden thing and nothing could surprise her. For the first time in an age I felt unencumbered.

Then the note. The flurry of countless voices, that unnamed choir, the convergence into the chord, pure and broadshouldered, rising with every passing moment.

"Hear it?" I asked.

"Hear what?"

"The music," I answered.

"There is no music, David."

I reached my hands toward her. She didn't move away. Only then did I realize they were insensate. I could see them at the ends of my arms. They turned when I turned them. The fingers moved when I moved them. But I could not feel them at all. I cupped her hands in mine.

"Can you feel that?" I asked.

"No," she said.

"Not at all?"

"No, David, you're not touching me."

I looked. I was touching her. The chord swept upward into sublime completion, the towering perch of its power.

"Now?"

She sadly shook her head. Then she pulled free, turned, and slowly moved into the sea.

"Sara?" I called after her.

She ignored me and began to fade into night.

"Sara?" More loudly.

Nothing.

"Sara!"

Only a trace of her remained.

"Sara!"

~ * ~

I bolted upright in bed. My skin felt sticky even though the temperature was mild and the air conditioner was working. I got up and threw on a pair of jeans. I grabbed the orange juice jug from the refrigerator and took it with me.

I sat at the top of the hill near the narrow pathway that meandered down to the rocks below. I had a headache, and the sound of the tidal surge was annoying. I swigged juice and tried to calm myself. Nightmares were frequent guests, and once I returned to my senses I would be okay. I simply had to focus on the real.

The real is not always salvation. The real is not even truth. Truth is an extrapolation of facts or premises, and is subject to as many interpretations as there are individuals presented with them. But in me, there seemed to be a single, recurring fact. And that fact invariably led to a single premise. And, as always, I arrived at the same truth.

Maybe I would never be a whole person. Maybe I was incapable of it, incapable of any sustained peace of mind. I wasn't sure I even knew how to begin.

~ * ~

Then the whales came.

A local expert said we had an entire pod, and that it was unusual for them to be migrating this late in the year for the Bering Straits from Mexico. No one knows exactly how the beaching happens, whether illness or lunacy causes them to lose their sense of direction, or whether it's merely a case of follow-the-leader, but they ran themselves aground, determined to stay there until they died.

Twenty beached whales was big news, and hundreds of volunteers congregated north of the Point Sur Lighthouse where the gray whales lay, keeping them wet and trying to push and cajole them back into the sea. In most cases they were successful, or at least successful enough for the pod to continue its journey northward.

One whale was especially stubborn. Monstrously large, he resisted all efforts to be moved, and even when he was shoved into deeper water, seemed content to wallow in the shallows until he drowned. So they nudged him farther out to sea, until he began to swim away, perhaps realizing that in order to die he would have to do so out of reach of his well-intentioned cousins.

South. Unnoticed, he swam in the opposite direction until there were no more people, and he beached himself again, this time on a sandbar about fifty yards from shore, where only a single person noticed. Me.

I saw him from my deck. At first I thought the disturbance was a school of fish until he rolled and a pectoral fin stuck out of the water as if waving goodbye. The music began. I shoved it aside and drank my coffee and told myself the rippling water was just a school of fish.

Even then, I knew. I was moving down the steps, across the yard, toward the top of the cliff, angling down the steep, crooked path. I don't think I fully realized what I was doing until I stepped into the water. The Pacific was cold, rousing me, and I stripped down to my underwear.

I swam to the sandbar afraid, not knowing whether he would struggle, attack, or move away. Instead he simply lay there, motionless except for the nudge of the breakers. I touched him, just to feel. His skin was rubbery, covered with patches of barnacles, but surprisingly warm to the touch. I began to stroke him, if for no other reason than the pleasure. Touching him was addictive, and I continued to stroke him over and over.

I began talking to him, whispering as if to a sick friend. Such a gentle old soul, unable or unwilling to move for reasons of his own. I didn't know if he liked it or not, but he kept the part I was touching exposed.

The music rose again then, and I let it come.

I closed my eyes and looked away, almost as if I could see a lone piper on some faraway hill. The note was joined, tremulous but sweet in the sun. The note soothed me, and I let the music come.

The chord. I drank it in, vulnerable still, but rendered unaware I was even touching the beast. I was alone in the music. The chord grew in intensity, though still tenderly, as a gentle reminder as to why it was there, whispering what I had always been loath to hear—that it was a part of me. The music belonged there.

The chord began its final motion, and I let it come. For the first time in a decade, I let it come. There was a millisecond when I hesitated, when I knew I could still force the power back, but something remarkable happened, something that had only happened in that odd and awful dream as my mother lay dead. I could see the music in my hands. And in my inward eye I saw a shadow, such a dark red-blue it was almost black, wavering slightly as if beneath the water, a shadowy form surrounded by white.

The shadow form was the illness, in complete contrast to the rest, running from the back of the beast's head all the way into a lung. I stretched my hands until I could cover both ends of the image, barely managing.

The chord rocketed upward, breaking free from any feeble confines I could have mustered, and I let the music come, the abandonment of a thousand instruments into perfect unity. I gasped with its ascension, and my self seemed to fall away, but there was no pain.

I could feel the power gather, and again I was afraid. It could rip me apart, but the music bathed me in the warmth of reassurance, and I did not pause. I let it go. The healing rushed from my hands like a mighty storm, pouring into the beast like a flood in a canyon, quickly covering everything in its path, but sealing every wound as it passed.

The rush spread, encompassing not only the area beneath my hands but both our physical selves. I began to see the dark area dwindle, revealing the green-white core of wholeness. And as it did, I could feel it, feel the completeness that was somehow a part of me, too.

I didn't want to stop. Even when the work had been done, I kept my hands in place. I felt movement beneath my hands, and the sweet song began to subside. I opened my eyes. I was shaking as I regained my outward senses.

The whale had swum away. I was alone.

Then, he returned, swimming two circles around me, brushing against me with a touch belying his mass. I reached to feel him a final time, now only the flesh-on-flesh contact of the physical world, before he moved into deeper water.

He was heading north. My breathing returned to normal, and the moment leaked away into the day. I waved after him.

"Be well," I whispered.

~ * ~

Every cubby along the coast had at least a dozen seafood restaurants, nearly all with names like The Catch of the Day, The Pirate's Cove, or The Angler's Inn, even though you could get seafood just as fresh in Denver.

There was something about the shore that made people think differently.

The best place for seafood in Ocean Park was called *Harry's*, and I liked it because they had a large covered deck where you could sit out on a pleasant evening and listen to a jazz trio while you ate.

Sara wore a dress. She looked beautiful, and not making a fool of myself was difficult. The dress was pale blue, knee-length with spaghetti straps. She wore a small gold crucifix, and I admired it for a moment because doing so also allowed me to trace the contour of her breasts without raising suspicion.

"I'm flat-chested," she said.

I snapped to like Lazarus. "What?"

"Sorry, but I am. I'm used to it."

"I was just looking at your necklace."

"I know. But we'd have gotten around to it sooner or later."

I really liked this woman.

"It's very nice. Memento?"

"Yeah. Sixteenth from my dad."

"He in San Francisco?"

She shook her head. "Under it. My parents are both gone."

"Sorry."

"It's okay. Yours?"

I paused. "My mother is. Over ten years now. It was...unexpected."

"So, we're both orphans."

"Seems that way."

We were served. Grilled shrimp in yellow rice with bay leaf for me and a platter for her. Amstel Light for both of us.

She took a bite, nodded that the food was good, and continued. "I don't think my parents planned to have any children. They married late, and I was a surprise. My father was forty-four and my mother was forty-two when I was born. I was loved, pampered in a lot of ways, but there was—I don't really know how to describe it—a lack of energy is probably right. My mother never took me shopping or told me secrets, and I was never Daddy's little girl."

"You know, I've thought about that, too," I said. "That I was an accident. My father wasn't around at all, and I'm sure my mother didn't plan to raise a child alone."

"What do you think that means?"

"I don't know. That the world can be a very capricious place, I guess."

"Doesn't make it any easier sometimes."

"No. It doesn't. So why medicine?"

She hastened her chewing to answer. "My father had a baby sister who was only about twenty years older than me, and I idolized her. Always took care of herself. Rode a motorcycle. Went diving in Fiji. Took me camping. Took me on trips with her friends and never treated me like I was in the way. She taught me the most important stuff I know."

"Like what?"

"Like the way a cactus blooms in the desert. Or how if you hold a glass of cherry Kool-Aid very still a hummingbird will come up and drink out of it. Or how to watch the sky for meteor showers. Or calm a horse. Or how there are a million kinds of magic in the world that most people take for granted."

Your life will be full of magic, David.

Something must have shown on my face.

"You okay?"

I nodded.

She waited a moment, and her voice softened. "Anyway, just before I graduated from high school I found out she'd been killed in a light plane crash somewhere off the coast."

"And you think you could've saved her?"

"Oh no. No one could have. I didn't become a doctor because of that. I became a doctor because she taught me the importance of finding a purpose. My magic."

My mind began to wander. Regardless of the definition, magic was the province of the naïve, those with the luxury of remaining ignorant. Call it charm, call it appeal, call it optimism. It wasn't magic. Real magic was dangerous, and the same caution I always carried just beneath the surface braced me.

She studied me, and her expression was thoughtful. She took another bite before saying anything.

"You don't believe me, do you?"

I sighed. I could do nothing, had no way to avoid the inevitable. "I don't believe in magic, no."

"Okay. I want to show you something after dinner."

~ * ~

I knew the place, of course. One of the best views in this part of the state. A natural overlook near the rain shadow of the forest, a promontory point near where the Little Sur River flowed into the Pacific.

We parked, and I followed her through a thick stand of Monterey pine to a massive rock landing two hundred feet above the water's edge. The sun had already submerged, and the moon cut a pale swath across the waves as far as the eye could see. A wide band of ridge and severe rock face covered the distance to the ground. The view was incredibly beautiful, but made by eons of evolution, not magic.

"You know this place?" she asked.

"Sure. It's where all the high school kids come to make out."

"Make out?" she teased.

"You know what I mean."

"Okay. But do you know the story?"

I didn't. I didn't even know there was a story. I shook my head.

The flattest part of the ledge was about sixty feet wide and twenty-five feet deep, smooth except for two melon-sized pockets about eighteen inches apart in the center, eroded by centuries of wind and rain. We sat there, and I watched as she gently rubbed her fingers along the indentations. It became very still, and then she spoke.

"A long time ago... hundreds of years, in fact, when the only people around were Spanish settlers, there lived a man and a woman named Paolo and Inez. They loved each other deeply, as much as any two people can love each other, and wanted to make a life together.

"One day Inez became very sick, and nothing seemed to work, and poor Paolo was driven to the breaking point with worry. So he brought her here. And he stood upon this very rock, holding the one great love of his life in his arms—and prayed."

"'Lord, please bring my sweet Inez back to me. For without her I will surely perish.'

"And the Lord answered. 'Consider this, Paolo. You may have a lifetime on earth with her or an eternity in heaven. You cannot have both.'

"Paolo didn't know what to do. He could keep her for fifty or sixty years and then lose her for all eternity, or he could give her up now and be with her for all eternity. Rationally, he knew that eternity was better than counted years, but in his heart of hearts he simply could not see spending his earthly life without her. Finally, he looked toward heaven and said—

"'I choose the lifetime with my beloved Inez.'

"And the Lord answered, 'So be it.'

"Inez got well. And they were married. They worked together, raised their children together, endured every trial together, and lived their lives in love.

"Then, when they were very, very old, Inez became ill again and died.

"Those days were filled with unbearable grief for him. Weeks went by, then months, then a year, then two. And he could find no relief from his agony. He was so bitter, you see, because not only did he miss her, but knew he would not see her in heaven.

"So he returned to this very place. And in a fit of rage he cried out, 'You have robbed me, Lord! I should not have had to make such a terrible choice! It's so unfair, and it's all your doing!'

"But the Lord remained silent.

"Poor Paolo just stood there, sick in heart, sick in body, trembling with such despair that he began to weep uncontrollably, until he thought he could weep no more.

"Then something strange happened. Somewhere from the deepest recesses of himself, he began to remember. He remembered the first time he ever saw her, how pretty she was. He remembered their first touch, their first kiss, how sweet it had been. He remembered each of their children being born, and how they had worked the land, good seasons and bad. He began to remember it all.

"He fell to his knees, his tears of sorrow becoming tears of shame and gratitude. And again he raised his voice toward heaven.

"'Thank you for my life, Lord. Thank you for the life you gave me with my Inez...'

"On and on he went, speaking only praise, recalling every wonderful memory and saying them aloud one by one, continuing into the night, and into the next day, and the next, never moving or faltering, until at last—and no one really knows how long it was—he finally fell peacefully asleep and died.

"And there waiting for him on the other side was his beloved Inez, looking as young and beautiful as when they first met.

"This is the spot where Paolo prayed. And these are the marks left by his knees."

I didn't speak for a long time, partly because I thought doing so would betray my emotion, but partly because I understood. Nothing existed without gain. However miniscule or mindless, intemperate or fleeting, there was always some measure of gain to be counted in all things. Perhaps that was what magic was—a divine, eternal particle of gain.

She was watching me expectantly.

"That was a great story," I said. "Where did you hear it?"

"I was winging it." She grinned.

I couldn't believe my ears. "You're kidding."

She shook her head with a laugh. "I made it up."

I laughed, too. "Unbelievable. You had me."

"It made you look at this place a little differently, didn't it?"

I thought for a moment. "Yes. It did."

Then she closed her eyes, and I watched the gentle curve of her cheek as she raised her face skyward. Her hair shifted silently, and a look of complete tranquility came over her.

"Believe what you want, David. The world needs magic in it," she whispered. "Otherwise we stop looking."

Nine

Everything is cause and effect. The moon, the tides—cause and effect. The wind, the waves—cause and effect. For every action there is an opposite and equal reaction. Things in motion tend to stay in motion. The world exists because of and for cause and effect.

That there is also spiritual cause and effect is understandable. Joy creates health. Sorrow creates suffering. An invisible chain reaction spreads from mind to body, from heart to soul. Unseen ghosts move throughout the psyche, sending tendrils throughout all we are, creating results as predictable as they are impersonally perfect.

I had never allowed myself the luxury of happiness. I didn't trust it. But as contentment began to take hold in me, I resolved to simply let it be.

The phone rang, interrupting my work. I was working on a gray whale, charcoal and white mottling, and the combination was trying my patience.

"Hello, you lovely creature," I said.
"David?"
"Who else would it be?"
"It's me."
"I know who it is."

"Sorry to bother you—"

"You're never a bother, Mrs. Felker. I've been meaning to tell you that."

She paused. "Have you been in my medicine cabinet?"

"No. Have you ever noticed just how many different shades whales have?"

"Aha. Wasn't that strange?"

"Very. What's up?"

"Eileen Bryson called. She's done a lot of business with me over the years."

"A good thing."

"Yes. She's very gung-ho about certain causes."

"I was telling Sara we're a wealth of social consciousness here."

"Oh. Hope you don't mind that I gave her your number. She's a doctor, you know."

"At the very least."

"Anyway, Eileen's involved in a summer day camp for challenged children. She thought I might be able to arrange for an artist to stop in and give a little tutorial. She asked for you. I told her you were extremely busy and weren't the type for this sort of adventure, but she insisted—"

"Sure, when?"

"—that I ask... what?"

"It sounds like fun. When do you want me to do it?"

A long pause. "How about next Tuesday morning?"

"Great. I'll be there."

Another pause. "Are you sure you're okay?"

"I'm fabulous. Besides, I owe you."

"I'll tell her then... Did I mention these are handicapped kids?"

"It'll be fine."

"Okay. I'll let you get back to work."
"Talk to you soon."
"David?"
"Yesss."
"Next Tuesday."
"I'll be there."

~ * ~

The old community center had been built as a WPA project back during the Depression. Its outer hull was mortared limestone quarried from the area, and the building looked like a prison. Bobby Vinton had played there in 1966. Now the center was used for aerobics, crafts classes, and dances for seniors.

The counselor who greeted me was a stout young woman fresh out of college who wore sweatpants and hiking boots and shook my hand like a longshoreman.

Six kids were there, ranging in age from ten to twelve, all with some form of cerebral palsy or MD, all in wheelchairs.

They all smiled alertly when I was introduced. They'd been given pads and crayons, so I moved to the blackboard. I didn't really have a game plan but thought of something simple.

"Art is easy when you learn a few tricks," I began. I drew a long, horizontal line with a couple of dips. "Can everyone do that?"

Everyone managed, and I waited until each was finished. "Good. Now draw exactly the same thing just below the line you just drew. Do your best to make it as much like the first one as possible, and try to keep the space between them as even as you can."

I drew the matching line and waited. "So what have you got?" I asked.

I could see awkward grins and shrugs, and no one knew. "Okay. Now connect the back of the two squiggly lines with a line that curves out. Do the same on the front. In the front, put a dot near the top and draw a thin little line at the bottom—"

"Snake!" The word was barely intelligible, but his crooked face beamed, and the rest of the class applauded. I felt like a celebrity.

I gave them a few more shortcuts and talked about proportion, and showed them that just about anything could be drawn using different sized smiles and frowns—everything from faces to cars to animals to scenery. I could see the looks of accomplishment as they began to make recognizable images, and the energy was palpable.

A little girl of nine or ten, with wavy brown hair and freckles and timeless eyes, caught my attention. Her dystrophy was advanced. Her legs were thin and nearly motionless, and she had full-length braces on each arm extending all the way to her palms.

I watched her surreptitiously as she cupped the weaker of her hands into the other, but her grip on the crayon still shook uncontrollably.

Afterward, as each child was rolled outside, I stayed behind and knelt beside her without attracting any attention. The counselor saw me and seemed to understand.

"I'm David," I said.

"Karen. I'm not very good at this."

"You will be once you have the right tools."

Connected to her chair was a foldaway tablet. I positioned it at an upward angle in front of her and locked it into place. I clipped on a piece of light construction paper. I had a long brush rigged with a clamp at the end instead of bristles. I attached a piece of colored chalk to the clamp lengthwise to create a wider stroke.

"What do you want to draw?" I asked.

She shrugged at first, a conditioned response, but she stared at the paper until a slight smile appeared.

"The beach," she said softly.

"One of my favorite things," I said.

I propped her weaker arm across the arm of her chair. I placed the stick in the stronger hand and used the other as a fulcrum. Then I shifted both into place so the end of the chalk could touch the paper and she would have some control.

"I know this will take some getting used to, but let's try it. Draw a line where you think the sand would end and the water would start."

She did. Managing the pressure took awhile but she soon had a wavy line the width of the paper.

"Good. Now put another line between the water and the sky."

"The horizon," she said.

"Yes."

We put in clouds and a couple of v-shaped birds, waves and rocks, dunes with tufts of grass, and a walkway. This took her several minutes, chewing her lip and her arm quivering from the constant force, but her eyes widened as the image began to take form.

"See," I said. "All along you were a chalk artist and didn't know it."

She beamed at me. "Yes. That's what I am."

~ * ~

I discovered sailing, or at least my version of it, my first summer here. I didn't have some deep-seated desire to harness the forces of nature, and I wasn't really adventurous. The truth was I didn't have the heart to put a noisy, smelly engine into the water, and I could make my way around the cove without doing myself or anyone else any harm.

I got the distinct impression, however, Sara had expected something a little more substantial, if not romantic, than what amounted to an over-sized dinghy with a mast.

"Oh," she said. "That's your boat."

The air was warm, the hour still early, and she wore baggy shorts with an armless Pink Floyd sweatshirt. At first we didn't talk at all. I'd glance over to find her looking outward, breathing it all in, or catch her watching me, with both of us smiling a little awkwardly afterward.

We caught a sheer heading back, and as we tacked to catch the wind we found ourselves together on the stern bench cupped like two spoons in a drawer. It was the first time we'd been this close, and I could feel her legs against mine, her back against my chest, her neck so close I could smell her shampoo.

Her nearness was wonderfully distracting.

We beached below my house. A large, flat rock with a crater in the center sat at the base of the cliff.

"This is the dent made when Paolo hurled himself off the cliff," I teased.

"Or at least where he stood and whizzed all those years," she answered.

We decided to take a picnic and hike into the forest. I grabbed some stuff out of the kitchen and threw it into a basket. We found a clearing along a creek and spread a blanket out in a trapezoid of light where the riparian vegetation was thin. Clusters of lupine and California poppies swayed in greeting, and the air smelled loamy.

I pulled out crackers, cheese, and some turkey breast, and a bottle of local zinfandel, which we drank from a couple of 49er mugs.

"The good china?" she said.

"For you, the best. And the cup will sit flat without spilling, too."

We sat on opposite ends with the contents between us, both acting casual and detached, as if this was commonplace, both knowing it wasn't. The wine was good, too sweet for true connoisseurs but perfect for me. We made little sandwiches with the crackers. We still didn't talk much, and I realized she'd been alone, too, because people accustomed to being alone don't talk when they eat.

"See that tree?" She pointed after a moment. "That's a Pacific yew. Know what it does?"

"Taxol," I said. "Anti-cancer drug."

"I'm impressed."

I took a bite and pointed to a stray redwood. "See that butterfly?"

"Yeah."

"It's a Smith's blue. Endangered."

"I'm impressed, the sequel," she said, smiling.

"I guess I've had too much time on my hands over the years."

"I hope to know what that's like."

"You have today."

"Yes. I have today. It's hard to believe there are still places this remote, this untouched here."

"It's protected, and not very accessible. This area didn't even have electricity until the fifties."

"I guess you draw a lot of inspiration from it."

I shrugged. "Nearly everything I do is from memory. I don't use models or paint live. Most of the time I do something long after the fact. Occasionally I take photographs."

She smirked. "Thanks, professor."

"Knew I should've used PowerPoint."

"That would've done it. But I think I understand. I can't really describe what I do. The training kicks in, and it just comes."

"Maybe we're just boring."

"But hopefully not to each other."

"Of course not."

She took a bite. "Would it be cloying if I asked you if you knew how good you really are?"

"What about you? Do you know how good you are?"

"But you don't have a frame of reference for that."

"Aha."

"It's not the same," she said.

"I know. I've just never been one of those 'one needs art to nurture the soul' group. There is music I love. There are books I love. I never miss a rerun of *The Ghost and Mr. Chicken*. But there are millions of people whose jobs are more important than mine. Including you."

"I think you underestimate yourself. I mean, people are willing to pay for your work. That must mean something."

"It does. It's very gratifying. I work very hard. And if people appreciate what I do, that's great. But sometimes I'd like to set the record straight—art doesn't have to mean anything. The value of art can be that it's just a pretty picture."

"I get that."

"Good. That makes two of us."

She piled a cracker high with turkey and cheese and popped it in her mouth, washing the bite down with a drink of wine. She looked at me over her mug.

"What about me?"

"What *about* you?"

"Would I make a pretty picture?"

I looked at her in the near-silence of the day, where shafts of light shone through the trees in uneven columns, and the water whispered sympathy for all things, and I wondered where the duplicity was, the cynicism, the uncanny knack to be anything at any moment without a second thought, but found none of it in her.

"Yes. A very pretty picture."

"So would you?"

"What?"

"Paint me."

"You're kidding."

"I don't look any worse than those Picasso women."

"Please," I said. "I meant I'm a lousy portrait artist."

She smiled her slow, mischievous smile. "Just as well. I couldn't afford you."

"I wouldn't do it for money."

"So when, then?"

She had me. And strangely, I wanted her to have me.

"You think you can sit still long enough?"

"Cheap shot, David."

"Okay. When are you off again?"

"I'm on call through Sunday. I'm supposed to be off Monday."

"We'll do it then."

"Seriously?"

"Yeah. Sure."

She reached across and grabbed me around the neck, our knees still a foot apart. The position was awkward, but I could feel her soft against me and relished the sensation. I reached a hand up and touched the back of her hair.

"You're such a nice man," she said lowly.

I closed my eyes. "You, too."

Then she began to giggle. After a moment, I began to giggle. Before the moment passed, we were both laughing silly. Before the moment passed, there was possibility.

~ * ~

The drive was long, and the day was stifling hot. I hadn't been back in four years, but the place didn't look much different. I used to go at least twice a year, if only to stare and wonder and grieve, but I would seethe for days afterward and poison would well in my muscles until I ached all over.

Today was different. Today she would have been sixty-two years old, still beautiful, still vital in mind and spirit and the ends of her nimble fingers. I placed a single flower against the stone and took a long look around. A few visitors and groundskeepers were around, but none close by.

My mind wandered, not to the past, but to the what-if dreams of today, those flash-forward hopes of what could have been. She would have been so proud of my success. She would've loved my house, sitting on the deck, listening to the music of the water. She would've enjoyed wandering the shops and bistros of the town, and meeting Mrs. Felker. She would have even treasured the story of the whale, if I could've found the courage to talk about it. And I was sure she would have liked Sara.

I looked down at my mother's grave. "I miss you," I said softly.

Yet there was more. I didn't know exactly what the more was or what form it would take, or if it would bring such awful heartache back, but as I waited for it, I knew the revelation would come.

The more came like a mother's kiss, warm and gentle, just as she had always been, just as she would have remained had she lived.

"Thank you, Mama," I whispered. "Thank you for giving me life, so I did not miss all the wonders I have seen..."

Ten

Painting her from memory would have been better, but she was determined to pose, and I really enjoyed having her there, so I just went with it. I decided to photograph her in various outfits to give us both some idea where we were headed. I set up with a plain backdrop and sheets draped over everything else.

The first had her in jeans and a flannel shirt. I gave her a flower to hold, which naturally drooped every time I got ready to shoot. I couldn't get her to smile without it looking forced, and I couldn't get her to move without her looking as if she was auditioning for some kind of local talent search.

The second was a simple print dress, and she was gorgeous in it. But I still couldn't get the right feel, so I just shot a roll of her standing, sitting on a stool, sitting on a bench, even looking back over her shoulder like in an old yearbook.

The third was in a white smock and stethoscope. Dr. Sara. The photo was awful. She looked so morose. Whenever she had that coat on all life seemed to disappear from her and she was someone else.

Afterward we ate. I needed time to develop the proofs, and we needed a break. We moved out onto the deck and drank a glass of the wine left over from the picnic. Dusk was approaching, and the air was cooler.

"How'm I doing?" she asked.

"I liked the dress."

"You mean the Shirley Temple look?"

"You look great in it, and those kinds of dresses never go out of style."

"You know why?"

"Why?"

"Because you don't have to wear underwear."

"That explains a lot."

She paused. "I was kind of hoping we could do my doctor suit."

I shook my head, perhaps too quickly. "We'd need divine intervention."

"Is that a crack?"

"I didn't recognize that person," I said seriously.

She became very quiet. A slight gust of wind blew through her hair, and I captured the image in my mind. "You can't give anything way," she said finally. "You can't look scared or the least bit out of control. Otherwise, you've had it."

"I understand."

She studied me for a moment. "Do you?"

"There's a lot at stake. Both of you can't be vulnerable."

"Yes," she said smiling. "I believe you do."

After a moment she looked to the horizon, and her body flowed after it. In the distance the sun was a great orange half-moon upon the water, scattering red and purple light all upon its wake. She watched and absorbed the sunset, and as she watched, I watched her.

I moved up behind her. My arms reached to move about her. They stopped short, and I couldn't seem to move them any closer. My hands hovered near her elbows for a moment, still unwilling to risk an uninvited touch. The note came, a melancholy horn, a lament for my caution. I pushed it back. Finally, I simply patted her.

"Come on."

~ * ~

We drank coffee and sat on the floor. I spread the proofs out in three piles on the cocktail table and dealt them like cards. It gave me an excuse to be close to her. Many were atrocious, and I'd already trimmed a lot. I didn't want to hurt her feelings, and some were simply bad photography.

Nothing looked natural in the first group, and even Sara laughed at the drooping flower. She gave the Dr. Sara proofs a long, plaintive look.

"Ye gods," she said. "Notify the next of kin."

"I told you I don't know how to work with models. I don't know how to give direction or anything like that. I can do this from memory."

She grabbed the last batch. She looked great in the dress, but the images were all contrived. She sighed heavily, so I pulled a single proof out from its hiding place. The photo showed her holding the hem of her dress in one hand with her head tilted gently to one side, her eyes closed. This one had not been posed. She'd been twirling around playfully, and the result was marvelous.

Her face brightened instantly, and she picked up the print.

"Yes," she said.

I set up outside. This part was redundant, but she wanted to stay and see it through. I put her in front of the huge water oak perched near the edge, its ring of shade providing the perfect containment for her, standing against a horizon of green and white sea.

Just as we got started, the most remarkable thing happened. Someone's dog ran into the yard. A pretty black-and-white Springer spaniel trotted right up to her, its tail stub wagging.

She stooped to pet the dog, her smile broadening so naturally, the hem of her dress backlit by the sun and brushing the ground.

I didn't have my camera. I rushed the outline onto the canvas. I could do all the detail later. I had the basics in less than two minutes. I worked frantically until I had all the rudimentary parts in place. The time I spent sketching couldn't have been more than four or five minutes. I was ecstatic and let my breath go in a single smooth stream. Finally, I looked up.

And she was gone.

My heart sank. Had I been so engrossed that she'd tried to get my attention and couldn't? I put my pencil down and walked toward the tree. I looked all around, seeing nothing. I looked over the bank—no woman, no dog.

Suddenly two hands reached out from behind and grabbed me, whirling me around and pulling me close. Our faces were inches apart, and we were both panting.

"I got it," I said.

"I knew you would," she answered.

Neither of us moved. The moment was there and far too potent to ignore. We could either plunge ahead or back away, and if we let the moment pass it might not come again.

Our faces reached for each other, eyes closing in unison, hands touching in a ballet of want and need. We kissed deeply, longingly...

~ * ~

We were holding each other in bed, aware night had claimed the air outside. Her head rested on my chest, her hand nestled just below my chin.

"I've never seen hands move that fast before," she said.

"What?"

"My portrait."

"Oh. Thank the dog."

"When will it be finished?"

"A week, maybe. I want to talk to you about that."

"Uh-oh."

"What uh-oh?"

"It sounded like an uh-oh to me."

"No. I just want to keep it."

"To sell?" she said, with a smile in her voice.

"No, of course not. To keep."

"Would I have visitation rights?"

"Anytime you want."

"And someday if we get all cranky and hostile, and can't stand the sight of each other and you decide to throw it off the cliff, could I have it?"

"Sure."

"Okay."

She shifted to look at me, and I could feel her breasts against my rib cage. I never wanted to move.

"David?"

"Yeah?"

"Is this a good thing?"

The rush of doubt I expected never materialized. "Yes. I believe it is."

"Do you believe in love at first grope?"

"I didn't have enough time to think about it between the first and the second grope."

"Okay. What about love at third grope?"

"I'll let you know after."

She sighed. "It's been a long, long time."

"Me, too."

"Wonder why that is."

I thought for a moment. "We've made things difficult for ourselves, the choices we've made."

"Maybe the really good stuff isn't supposed to be easy."

"Maybe." I wondered what she would do if she had any inkling as to how truly different we were; how I shrank from what she embraced, how I fled from the responsibility she coveted. "Was it worth it?" I asked.

"The wear-and-tear?"

"Yeah."

She lifted her hands, studying them, almost as if they weren't connected, as if they belonged to someone else.

"Yes," she said finally. "I know there are thousands of people who do what I do. Many better. But to have some tiny, insignificant part of the power to heal...You know, sometimes when I'm working on someone it's almost as if my hands have a mind of their own. They dance when they touch. They love when they touch. They—"

"Make music," I said.

I could feel her eyes upon me even as I looked away, past the ceiling, past the sky, past the nether regions of space into the infinite hollow of life.

"Yes," she said. "That's it exactly."

I pulled her close again. "I know."

~ * ~

Estelle Pauling felt the sharp jolt of pain, and that was good. Pain meant her head was starting to clear and she was still alive. She noticed the chart at the end of her bed, the cheap institutional curtains that blacked out the morning, the stand with the IV, the monitors.

The veins in her arms were nearly collapsed, and she felt the IV needle in the back of her hand, making her wince.

The footsteps outside the door were quicker than usual. She smiled to herself and closed her eyes again.

Sara crept into the room and walked directly to the foot of the bed and silently retrieved the chart. She glanced at the bag hanging from the stand. Time for a changeover. Maybe the morphine was helping. She checked the old woman's arms. Both were thin and bare and covered with small bandages where IVs had been replaced and moved far too often.

"You're in a good mood."

The thin, airy voice startled her, but she didn't show it. "Now what makes you think that, Mrs. Pauling?"

"You don't scowl as much."

Sara looked at her and smiled. "I'll remember that. You want to go home today?"

"Have to. Been here so long this time I'll never get that old man straightened out."

"Well, just make sure he brings you back for chemo."

"He'll be back in here before that if my house is a wreck." She shuddered again in pain. Sara checked the chart without expression.

Please, Mrs. Pauling. Just go to sleep and don't wake up.

"Time for a booster," Sara said. "I'll send the nurse right in."

Mrs. Pauling nodded and forced a smile. "Dr. Rembert?"

Sara turned at the door. "Yes, Mrs. Pauling?"

"Who is he?"

Sara grinned and shook her head. "Just get some rest."

She went straight to the nurse's station and wrote new instructions. She looked at the duty nurse and lowered her voice.

"I need help with this."

"Yes, doctor."

"Discharge. Her husband is old, and I don't want either of them to have to wait around. Please have the ambulance here and her in it by the time he arrives."

"Of course, doctor."

~ * ~

The door began to close. I saw my hand reach to stop it, and I knew then I'd finally lost my mind.

It had begun so innocently.

"San Jose," she said.

"Eleventh largest city in the U.S.," I answered.

"I have to go to a medical conference. Just for the day. Want to ride along?"

Hospitals still terrified me, but I wanted to be with her. "No icky stuff, right?"

"No icky stuff."

"I guess we should take my car."

I could hear her smile through the phone. "Let's."

We got an early start and ate breakfast on the way. The day was blustery and overcast, but we enjoyed the drive.

San Jose is in a bowl where Silicon Valley leans against the Diablo Range. San Jose Medical Center was downtown, and I let her out and parked. I spent a couple of hours in a lounge reading the *San Francisco Chronicle*.

Afterward I walked down to the campus of San Jose State. The college was thinly populated this time of year, and I wandered over to San Pedro Square. I loved the old archway and the outdoor dining, scattered conversation, and saw a couple of kids playing guitars in front of a coffee shop.

I bought a cup of regular coffee without all the affectations, and I wondered if anyone really knew just how good a plain cup of coffee could be.

The air began to smell like rain so I started back. It would be time to pick her up soon.

The seminar was in the third floor conference room. The hospital was a difficult environment to be in, a place where every sound and odor called to the music, and naturally I got lost. I wandered the corridors trying to read the directions on the walls, loath to approach anyone. Staff, patients, and visitors ignored me, and I let them.

I don't know how I managed to arrive at the sealed double doors with the wire-glass translucent windows and large buzzer, but I recognized the entrance to the Psychiatric Ward.

I stood there for a moment. I could almost sense the misery contained within, and I could not linger long. As I turned to move away I heard a loud crash from the other side, followed by an anguished wail. An attendant quickly exited, giving me no more than a passing glance. The door began to close...

I slipped inside and approached the door where the commotion was. In the middle of the dayroom floor was a spilled container with flowers and water scattered about. I peeked in without being seen.

Five people circled the wreckage in as many orbits and states of vexation. An old woman, perhaps the offender, hovered nearest wringing her hands. Two younger women shuffled by, one clutching a doll and another pointing down crying, "Mess! Mess!" An old man danced a two-step toward the spill and away, and there was a boy, not even out of his teens, who wore a helmet obviously for his own protection and made airplane noises as he moved in wide circles with his arms outstretched.

The mayhem was unbearably pointless. The music stirred within me, so gravely now. My heart moved to hear the note weep for those whose pain had no visible source. The notes flurried a dirge. And the chord came like a requiem mass for the touched and untouchable.

I began to cry. Tears were foolish, but I couldn't seem to help myself. No one noticed until the airplane boy flew up to me and stopped, looking at me plaintively, the top of his helmet near my chin.

His lower lip began to tremble. "Are you sad, mister?"

I wiped tears from my eyes and shook my head. "No."

Without warning he fell against my chest and flung his arms around me. "Don't be sad," he whispered. "It doesn't help."

So I let the power come. I let the music swell into full life until I could not contain it and the chord swung wide its gates. I reached and cupped the back of his head. I let the healing course from my hands. The music enveloped us, and the movement around us stopped. The others simply watched.

Then, without a sound and without doubt, they silently approached and moved within my grasp. I ushered them in. One by one I embraced them all...

~ * ~

The attendant returned with a mop and bucket, muttering to himself. He took one look and stopped in his tracks, the mop handle slipping from his fingers and slapping the floor.

All five sat serenely, alive, awake, and unmistakably whole. The airplane boy walked up and calmly lifted the mop from the floor.

"Where have you been, Leon? We were starting to worry about you."

Eleven

Sara and I danced on the deck. Songs from the forties played on NPR for a couple of hours, and most of the tunes were languid and slow. I loved the music. I loved how the parts came and went, how a clarinet would release to muted brass, becoming the same thing, how melody and rhythm combined and how I could even anticipate changes.

Everything I heard spoke to me in some sweet, exotic language. My senses had become heightened, and I seemed to be aware of every nuance of sound. No matter the melody, the message was always the same.

Love.

Engrossed in each other we danced, eyes closed, our hips pressed tightly together, gently swaying in unison. I could feel the entire length of her body to my knees, and I swam in the sensation.

"You never told me you liked to dance," she whispered.

"That's because I don't."

"No?"

"No."

"Why not?"

"Because I'm terrible at it."

"I hadn't noticed."

"That's because you're still in the infatuation stage. Reality comes later, and after that, disdain."

"I so love your optimism."

"See what I mean? Disdain already."

"You," she said, squeezing even more tightly against me. "So, then. Which of my faults are you overlooking?"

"All of them."

She thumbed me in the ribs and started to kiss me, but her beeper went off. She snatched the thing from the table and retrieved the cell phone from her purse. I gave her room.

"When did they bring her in? Okay, ask Dr. Evans to up her dosage. Right. I'll be there."

She was noticeably distracted.

"Trouble?" I asked.

She shrugged. "Mrs. Pauling. A patient. She's terminal. I tried to make her comfortable enough to die at home. Obviously that didn't work."

"You need to go?"

She looked at me blankly, and I watched the expression evolve into a nod of apology. "Yeah. I'd better. Sorry."

"It's your job," I said.

"No," she said sadly. "It's more than that."

~ * ~

I sat alone at my mother's piano, a drink making a mess through the napkins I'd folded as a coaster. The liquor was Scotch, and I never drank. I really didn't like hard alcohol much. I'd never acquired the taste. I thought drinking was a bad habit for weak, ineffectual people.

I was on my third.

Sara's portrait hung on the wall like a fine glimmer of promise. I stared at the painting long enough to make sure it wasn't going to move. I was feeling sorry for myself. I could never be what she already was. I could never be as brave, as certain. I would always be bound to the wan insurgency of dread, the intractable summons of panic.

I'd learned long ago a believable lie was sometimes better than the truth when the truth was too agonizingly bizarre to share.

She already gave me grief about my solitary ways, and I had already begun lying. "Can't we spend a quiet evening at home?" "It's too crowded this time of year." "I like it when it's just the two of us."

Oh, Sara. Sometimes people die, and it's my fault.

I could never tell her. How would I begin? How would I stop? How afraid would she become?

The note came unexpectedly. Not because I was morose or sullen, nor because I was so self-absorbed I was incapable of common pleasure, nor even because I was so predisposed to misery I actually welcomed it, although they were all true.

I was in love with her, and the feeling scared the hell out of me.

The note hung there, patiently waiting. I reached down and found the tone on the piano. I had no way to duplicate the trill, but I rocked my fingers between two notes. I actually found part of the chord, although ten fingers were not nearly enough.

The music stopped. I waited. Nothing happened. So I found the note again, my foot on the sustain pedal. The music followed. I quavered thirds and fifths. It echoed. I played my part of the chord. It answered.

Then the music began first. I accompanied. And I began to feel my spirits lift from the age-old burden. I continued for over an hour, with the note and its ilk, then to the chord, sometimes in unison, sometimes overlapping, sometimes themes and variations; sometimes I would retreat to the note and hold that tone while the internal music floated toward the chord, and we would usher it in together. The duet was glorious. Simply music.

Finally I stopped, until the last sustained chord faded into every corner of the room and every corner of myself, and I was able to sleep peacefully.

~ * ~

As much as I hated to admit such a thing, I needed to feel life around me. The season was in full swing at the beach, and I needed the commotion, the purposeless urgency of noise. The beach was crowded, and no one seemed aware of anything beyond his own private space. I moved through the throng of twos and threes, and no one gave me a second look.

Then I saw her. A woman, middle-aged but weary and spent, white limbs poking out of an ill-fitting swimsuit, hat and sunglasses obscuring most of her features, her face expressionless as she wheeled her daughter from the walkway a few feet into the sand, parking her beneath an umbrella.

The girl in the wheelchair was Karen, the little girl from the day camp. She smiled at her mother gratefully, a blanket over her legs and a couple of books in her lap.

I stopped. People milled around without noticing. No tragedies existed in mid-summer.

Karen read for awhile and talked with her mother. She talked with animation and enthusiasm, her mother listening patiently, nodding and occasionally responding, habitually adjusting the blanket on her daughter's legs every so often. I almost gathered enough momentum to speak to them. Instead I stood back and watched.

After about a half hour Karen began to nod off. Her mother had been waiting, her patience rewarded. She got up and moved toward one of the concession stands, looking back every few feet.

A retaining wall stood near the walkway, with people camped all along it between the girl and her mother's line of sight. I couldn't believe what I was thinking.

No. Turn around. Go home.

A stray Frisbee came sailing in. I kicked it along the beachside of the wall a few feet. I found the errant players about thirty yards away looking for the disk on the opposite side.

I had to be quick but didn't know if I could be that quick. I stooped and tossed the Frisbee a couple of feet behind the wheelchair. It stuck in the sand and I crab-walked over to it, looking around to see if anyone was looking. No one was.

I found her mother. Fourth in line. She stood there, hand on hip, impatient, looking back in our general direction but seeing only the top of the umbrella.

I called to the music even before I moved. Eyes open and in the hot light of day, it came. The notes, the chord, the swelling chorus. The notes came gently, and all other sound was blotted out. I knelt behind the chair, seeing she was still asleep, the Frisbee between the back wheels. I pretended to tie my shoe.

I took a breath. I would be exposed for a time, but I tried to ignore my vulnerability. I closed my eyes and reached out my hands and pushed the chord upward to its most lavish summit. It came, and I was there in the music, in the purposeful cloud of inner oblivion. I gently took hold of her ankles.

I hastened to let the power go. The music rushed from me. Just as quickly the sounds of surf and scattered voices returned, and the healing was done.

I picked up the Frisbee and moved away. I walked until I was across the wall and hidden in the motion of bodies. I waited.

A few minutes later the woman trudged through the sand carrying two drinks. At the same time Karen stirred as the weight of her head dipped her face into the sunlight.

"I'm here, honey," her mother called. And when Karen looked her mother held the drinks aloft, still fifty feet away.

The moment took on a life of its own. First came Karen's surprise and nervousness as she felt the sudden tingling. She wiggled her toes. They worked. She dipped them into the sand, bringing them up, scattering the grains, and repeating it all, as if such a simple act were astounding. She slowly shook her head in doubt, but pulled the blanket aside. She pushed herself to her feet, a look of puzzled exhilaration crossing her face as she did.

Her mother moved along, head down, unaware, by rote.

Karen took a single step in her direction. Then another. Then another, her face brightening with every movement.

Finally her mother looked up, stopping in her tracks, her mouth agape as the drinks fell to the sand and onto her sandals. She didn't care. She covered her mouth with her hands. She mouthed the words 'Dear God'.

Karen laughed aloud. She was proud, unfettered, and undenied. She hobbled forward, one wobbly step after another, each more sure than the last. Her mother dropped to her knees, just as she had all those years before when her daughter had taken her first steps, only now with her face contorted in the sudden cleansing of her broken heart.

Karen hastened the last few steps, nearly tripping in delight, triumphant as she flung herself into her mother's waiting arms.

"Did you see, Mama! Did you see?"

Her mother sobbed, the weight of those years collapsing into sublime frailty. "I see, baby. I see."

~ * ~

A simple painting sat on the easel, a remembrance of our picnic, a forest glen blanketed with wildflowers and far brighter colors than I normally used. The hands were hidden in a butterfly against a Pacific yew. Mrs. Felker's mouth was twisted into a smirk, and I was a little sensitive about it.

"I'm glad you're happy," she said.

"Oh please. How many times have you told me to explore new ideas? All my themes are there. Anyone who knows me can tell I did it."

"It's just that I've never seen anything like this from you before. All this color... it looks like Oz."

I blew through my cheeks and reached to take the painting. "It's not finished."

"I didn't say you shouldn't pursue it."

"You made your point." I pouted.

She smiled and patted my knee like she would a kid. She shifted in her chair, shifting modes. She took a sip of tea, peered at me over her reading glasses, and lowered the inflection of her voice. This meant money.

"San Francisco really kicked things up a couple notches," she began. "I've been getting inquiries from all over. The rumor mill has it there isn't a lot of your work available, and I haven't discouraged that."

"Of course you haven't."

"Rothschild's in New York has made an offer. They're not sure about the east coast, but they're convinced European markets would devour your style. They have obviously surmised you're of Irish descent and put a certain amount of stock in that."

"I don't know what that means."

"Nor do I. What they think it means is that you are a throwback. A pre-Modern Romantic who just happened to have the misfortune of being born in California."

"What do they want?"

"Twenty pieces."

"I don't—"

"—have twenty pieces? I told them that already, even though we both know it's bushwa. This could be huge, David."

I grinned. "I'll see what I can scrape up."

"You do that." She paused for effect. "Not that a fortune and the adoration of the entire art world would matter."

"Mrs. Felker, I'd do it for free just to see you once a week."

She smiled genuinely. "Of course you would."

We let the moment light. "Besides," I said finally, "I want to get back to the new series."

"What new series?"

I nodded toward the painting of the meadow. "Next I'm moving into forest animals, like in *Bambi*."

"Great," she said. "I'll call Hallmark."

~ * ~

I went to meet Sara at 11:30. I was tired, but I hadn't seen her in three days. I would've preferred meeting her at my house. I don't know why, but I don't feel completely comfortable in her apartment. I guess it has something to do with territoriality. Even when we want company we also want to control the who, the when, the where, and the how long.

I took some baked spaghetti and French bread. I heard her old bug roar around the curve a half mile away. She pulled up, got out, and smiled at me.

"I left you a key."

"I just got here," I said, hugging her.

"Sure you did. I wouldn't have left the key if I didn't want you to go in. Besides, I hid all those tapes with me and the football team."

"There goes dinner and a movie."

I nuked the spaghetti, baked the bread in the toaster oven, and set the dinner out to let the molecules decelerate for a few minutes. Sara threw a couple of plates and a roll of paper towels on the table, and headed for the shower.

"Wanna watch?" she said over her shoulder.

"I'll finish setting the table," I said.

"Suit yourself."

I waited until she left the room and got a painting out of my car. I'd done it as a surprise for her.

She came out with her hair wet, wearing a terrycloth robe so threadbare it was almost transparent. She sat beside me, and I pulled out the painting. I had framed it and put it in a large bag, but an imbecile could tell what it was. She acted surprised when I handed it to her.

"I have something for you."

"Really? Goody."

She opened it as if it was a treasure map. I had painted her at work, white coat and stethoscope. Her eyes were bright like the first time I saw her, and she had just a hint of a smile. Her arms were folded across her chest. And under the left pocket of her topcoat, near her heart, hidden in contrast to a natural wrinkle, were a pair of folded hands.

"I tried to capture the sobriety of the office, without all the sobriety."

Her face turned red. She looked at me like a schoolgirl after her first kiss, and reached her arms around me. I wallowed in her scent, and we held each other for a long time.

"Thank you," she said.

"You're welcome."

"Why would you spend so much time on this?" she asked gently.

I didn't respond right away. In the end my soul spoke. "You've brought grace into my life," I whispered.

"Amen," she answered.

Twelve

Karen's recovery didn't make the news. Nothing hit the paper, and no human interest stories appeared on local television. I'd even milked Mrs. Felker for all the local gossip. I still wasn't satisfied. I found where she lived and watched as she came out of the house. Something was terribly wrong. Her mother was pushing her in her chair.

Heavy-hearted, I followed her to the doctor. I waited until she came out. When she did, I couldn't help grinning like a fool. She walked to the car with all the normalcy of her age. Modern therapies, no doubt. The last I saw of her she was kicking a soccer ball in her front yard.

I don't know if true redemption can ever be earned, if that delicious ease of mind and spirit can truly be achieved by one's own hand. Perhaps in parcel, but perhaps real redemption must be gifted, and comes as unexpectedly as undeserved.

What I do know is redemption cannot be properly honored without requital. There is no havingness without givingness, no real value to its inheritor except his heart becomes a mirror where a wall once stood.

I was driving through another neighborhood. My mind raced. The evening had grown too dark to see the numbers, almost too dark to breathe. I kept telling myself

I was doing it for her. I was, in part, but I was also doing it for me. I needed to feel. I needed to love.

This was the oldest development in the area. All the houses were small and looked much the same, and the neighborhood reminded me of home. I found the house at the end of the street. The name was on the mailbox, and I caught part of it in my headlights. A light was on in the front room, but the rest of the house was dark. A single street lamp illuminated parts of four or five houses, most of them completely dark by now, silent.

I parked as if I belonged there. I walked straight across the yard to the door and looked in. I heard the laugh track to a sitcom on television, and its light pulsed in and out of the box. An old man was sitting in a recliner sound asleep.

A window unit blasted its version of cold air even though the door stood open. The screen door wasn't locked. I opened it like a thief, prepared to bolt at any moment.

I moved deliberately across the floor. He didn't stir. I moved down the hallway. The house was nearly pitch-black, but I could see the outlines of several other doors and a table along one wall. Creeping along, I found a bathroom and a spare bedroom that had been converted into a sewing room. Only a single door was left. It had to be.

The odor of medicine and slow decay greeted me as I opened the door. I walked straight to the side of the bed, knowing I was more likely to be caught trying to sneak.

She lay motionless, her torso propped up on pillows, her arms lying still at her sides as if laid out at an old-fashioned wake. Her breath rattled in drug-induced stupor.

A chair had been placed beside the bed. The old man's vigil, and I imagined him there. I thought of how a lifetime shared would command such attention without a second thought. How faith perpetuated by such commitment would create an environment where even the dark specter of death was preferable to the physical separation that would come soon enough.

I breathed in slowly through my nose and folded my hands near my lips in concentration. I could feel my own skin with the tips of my fingers, and the music began to rouse.

The note, a distant Pan. Wavering and growing. The chord, perfectly now. I could feel its power and its eagerness. I closed my eyes and reached, and it soared upward at the same instant—

"Who are you?"

The music exploded inside my head, great chunks breaking apart and scattering. My heart pounded two beats a second, and my eyes flew open.

She was looking at me, groggy, unfocused, afraid. I pushed the music aside, feeling the swell of compassion, touching her frail arm with no power other than my own, and patted her gently.

"A friend," I whispered. "Please trust me."

She smiled weakly. "You certainly are a pretty boy." Then she closed her eyes and faded.

I reclaimed the chord, finding new confidence and the presence of mind to pull in every stray note until the music was intact. Once that was done, the chord surged, pure and powerful and incendiary. I closed my eyes again and took another breath.

As with the whales, my vision altered. Islands of darkness infected a sea of green, too numbered to grasp. I woke to it, seeing in the music the light of bright white, a swirling nebula that became a single, pulsing strand.

I felt it in our contact. The power billowed inside me and poured down my arm, bathing every cell it touched in heat and love. The healing continued even as I became aware of the passage of time, the seconds ticking off, five... ten... still not weakening, still not emptying me, until the task was done.

I opened my eyes to regain my bearings. The music curled into its secret place. Everything was as it had been. She showed no outward sign except that her breath was stronger now, rhythmic and sure. She still slept.

I left the room, moving back down the hallway and across the living room. The old man was still dozing, the same show still on television. The clock on the wall said less than ten minutes had passed. I quietly closed the door behind me and walked to my car. The night was calm and unmoving. I turned on the classic rock station. The end of "Hey Jude" was playing, and I sang along. Loudly.

~ * ~

The shift had been relatively easy, but the lack of sleep made her punchy and on-edge. She hid away in her office, reading an update on interferon.

Her thoughts strayed, so often these days. A quiet, gentle man in a house by the ocean, and the possibility of a future she'd dared not consider. She was not afraid to love. She was not afraid to want. She was terrified to need.

Her thoughts turned to those things over which she had at least some control. She thought of the patients she'd seen that night. The old man had been lucky. There had been no delay. She'd opened him up, staunched the bleeders, sutured the tears. He'd live to jaywalk again. A young woman with sun-poisoning, self-inflicted but still painful. She'd survive and would be blistered again within a few weeks.

And the boy. He'd gotten hit with a baseball during a Little League game. Just a bad hematoma and an overnight stay where he could be doted on.

"Are you my doctor?" he'd asked, wide-eyed.

"I am until your doctor gets here. Is that okay?"

He grinned. "You're hot."

"And you're a flirt."

She propped her feet on her desk and draped a damp cloth across her forehead. Three-thirty, and all was well. The rest of her shift would probably be quiet. Most of the people who were doing something stupid enough to hurt themselves had done so by this time.

She heard the click, the early-warning of the P.A. system. She was on her feet and in motion before the announcement came.

"Dr. Rembert. One-ten. Code blue. One-ten. Code blue. Stat."

She pushed aside the surge of adrenaline. One-ten was the baseball boy. His EKG monitor was flatlining, the tone dull and monotonous, and he lay rigid and cold. A nurse already had the defib unit charging with the paddles in the air.

"What the hell happened?" Sara barked, grabbing the paddles as a nurse bared the boy's chest.

"No warning," the nurse answered.

The boy's parents stood off to the side, their faces grim and taut, mirroring each other. An attendant gently moved them out of the way.

Sara placed the paddles center and left. "Clear!" The jolt rocked the boy's body, but he quickly settled back into lifelessness. The monitor tone was desperately annoying.

"Again!" No response. She increased the intensity.

"Again!"

"*Again!*"

~ * ~

The phone rang. My eyes were on fire. I saw the blurred numbers on the clock: 4:32. Something was wrong. I answered, fumbling the receiver.

"David?"

Her voice cracked. I sat up. "Sara? What is it?"

There was a slight hesitation. "I need you."

"I'll be right there."

Fifteen minutes later I was standing at her door. No lights were on, unusual for Sara. She must've been watching for me because she opened the door before I knocked.

She looked terrible. She wasn't crying, but her face was red and puffy. Without a word she reached for me. I held her, and we moved inside.

"What's wrong?" I asked.

She bit her lower lip and shook her head. She was fighting for composure. Her eyes moistened, but she did not cry, and she did not speak until she was sure her voice would not break.

"Sorry to roust you like this."

I moved her to the sofa, and we both sat, facing each other. "Tell me what happened."

She stared down at her hands, opening and closing them. "Sometimes my hands are useless. Sometimes things happen I just can't fix."

I felt every raw bit of her pain, acutely and precisely. I clasped her hands and let her continue.

"A kid came in last night. God, what a sweet little boy. He'd been hit in the head with a baseball. Routine. A mild concussion. Some bruising. He didn't even have all his permanent teeth yet."

Her lips started to quiver, and she bit down in vain. Tears pooled and threatened to spill.

"A blood clot came loose. It lodged in his heart. There was nothing I could do, and he... just... died..."

I knew her sorrow so intimately, so deeply—how utterly enveloping the grief was. I wanted to shelter her from the cloying pain and banish it. She couldn't fend off the weight of it for long. Suddenly, she pitched forward against me and cried.

"What a stupid, stupid way to die."

I held her as if both our lives depended on it. Maybe, in some odd sense, they did. Maybe this was the only chance either of us would have. I couldn't believe that of her, but it was true for me. I silently thanked God for her and stroked the back of her head.

"I know it's hard. But you didn't fail. Not really."

"No?"

"No. You only fail if you give up—if you quit. And you won't do that."

"No, I won't ever quit."

"Do you know why?"

She sniffed. "Because I'm stubborn."

"Because it's your magic. And the world needs magic in it."

She looked at me then. Her eyes were so large, her cheeks glistening. I knew at that moment how much being without her would hurt.

"I love you," she whispered.

"I love you, too."

Again we embraced. And the music gently flowed into being, now as a comfort, delivering me to its goodness. I wrapped my fingers over her shoulders. The note. Love. The notes twirled and blended. Love. The chord emerged like a rainbow from the clouds. Love. It lifted, elevating us both to its untainted, unalloyed core. Love. I gave it all to her. Love...

~ * ~

We held each other in the muzzy fog of near-sleep, both exhausted. At the edge of the shades I could see the faint complexion of daybreak. I stroked a spot between her shoulder blades.
"David?"
"Hmmm?"
"Are you okay?"
"Yeah, why?"
"You feel warm."
"I thought that was the general idea."
"No, you feel feverish."
"Probably just from being up so long."
She giggled lowly. "No pun intended."
"Please."
"David?"
"Hmmm?"
"When we were making love..."
"Yeah?"
"Did you hear something?"
"Like what?"
"I don't know. I could've sworn I heard music."
"Go to sleep."

~ * ~

She was on the Internet, reading about a new technique to sterilize organs during surgery when Mike Perkins called. They'd been in med school together, never really friends, but now they were colleagues, practicing different medicine in different parts of the state.

"We didn't get your registration form back," he said.

"Yeah, going to sit this one out," she answered.

"What, and pass up all those great home movies of leeches during microsurgery?"

"Hard to believe, isn't it?"

"So, how is the wasteland?"

"Busy. Too busy this time of year."

"Me, too. It's killing my golf game."

"I'll bet."

"Sorry I won't see you. I'm going just to see the Grail. Who knows, maybe the image of Moses will appear in a bedpan or something."

"What are you talking about?"

"You didn't hear?"

"What?"

"The same day we were at the head trauma conference. Five psychiatric patients had some kind of spontaneous recovery. I can't believe you didn't hear about it. It was big news."

"So, some chemicals kicked in."

"*Nein, mein doktor.* These people had completely different pathologies. One was autistic, for God's sake. All with complete recovery on a chemical level. All at the same time."

"That is strange. What do they think happened?"

"Nobody knows. And the patients aren't talking."

She thought about that day. Absolutely nothing out of the ordinary she could remember. "Well, if you find out what it was send me a couple of gallons."

"Will do."

Thirteen

I had the worst cold I could remember. I was so congested I couldn't breathe, so achy I only moved under threat of wetting my bed. Sara was determined to help. Of course, I was a wonderful patient.

"Go away."

"Roll over," she said firmly.

"Not now, honey, I have a headache."

"Do it, David."

I turned over before I looked. It should've been the other way around.

"What the hell is that?"

"A hypo. What does it look like?"

"It looks like a prop from *Ben Hur*."

"House calls aren't cheap. Consider yourself lucky."

"So where are you going to put that thing?"

"In your butt, lover, unless you flinch. Then, who knows?"

"Will it hurt?"

"A little sting."

She was right. A little sting, just before it felt like a hammer and chisel. "Ow!"

"It's over now. Drink your juice."

"Yes, doctor."

She shook her head. "What a baby."

"I'm delirious and in agony. What do you expect?"

She packed her bag. "I expect you to ignore my advice and do things your own way so you'll be sick twice as long as necessary."

"Good as done."

She sat on the edge of the bed for a moment and stroked my hair away from my forehead. It was plastered with sweat.

"Seriously, if you get worse, call me."

"I will."

She got up to leave. "You get well enough to go out, we're going shopping."

"For what?"

"New sheets."

"What's wrong with these?"

"They're gray."

"So?"

"They used to be white."

She smiled and left. I nodded after her. Then I nodded off.

~ * ~

I didn't like to shop. Obvious reasons existed why I tried to avoid hubbub of every kind. There was also my gender, a fact I could not change and did not wish to defend. But more than that, I just didn't like to look for things. Instead, I waited until I really needed or wanted something and then I went directly to where I could find it and bought it, usually on the Internet.

We were in the linen section, and Sara was plundering for sheets. She didn't seem to enjoy shopping, either, but she did seem to enjoy trying to find something she believed had been hidden to spite her.

"Can I snoop around the music department?" I asked.

"You don't need my permission," she answered.

"I know, but you're doing this for me."

She frowned in my direction. She was doing that a lot lately. "Shoo. But if you don't like what I pick out I don't want to hear about it."

"I'll find you in a little while."

It was Saturday and very crowded, and I should've known better. The place was abuzz, and people milled in all directions, and canned music played in the background, and I felt woozy.

The note came uninvited, louder than usual, resolute. Again, my vision changed. It surprised me, not because of the insight itself, but because of the proximity. I was nowhere near anyone.

I became dizzy, but I didn't move away. Instead, I concentrated.

My eyes came to rest on a woman, and I could see the dark red-black glow of arthritis in her elbows encompassed by a thin green halo. A man across the way had a small tumor on his kidney, dark gray with the same healthy rim. I was doubtful he was even aware of it. Another had several black spots in his brain with uneven filaments snaking out from each, still blanketed in mossy light. He moved slowly, affectedly, nearly shuffling along.

I continued to look and saw infirmity of every kind in dusky threat, though encompassed by the thin strips of hope.

All the while the note persisted, so familiar I wasn't completely aware of it. As the note rippled into the chord, all ambient noise seemed to dissolve until I was left alone in the music with no sight nor sound, impression or expression, except those now revealed. I felt its upward turn and held it there. I didn't know if I was even capable as I moved toward the woman with arthritis. I squeezed by her, barely making contact as the chord rose.

She did not look at or acknowledge me. And with the chord aloft, I began to move down each aisle, merely brushing past people as I went. No contact lasted more than a moment, and I continued row-after-row, giving only the briefest of nudges, touching everyone as I passed and feeling the heat leave me as a lucent balm was cast.

As I moved, I saw those who were whole and those who were not and touched anyone with the spattered tar of disease. I must have touched twenty-five or thirty people, none mindful of the connection except for an occasional passing glance.

Finally, I paused breathless and exhausted near the front. The music dwindled into the blithe bustle. I surveyed the store. No signs showed mass renewal, but the blighted images were gone. One person moved an arm to a shelf and back with renewed strength. Another flinched and removed a hearing aid, only to find the device was no longer necessary. Some stepped more spryly with a look of curiosity on their faces, while others breathed more deeply, laughing impulsively under their breaths.

Heads and eyes cleared. Muscle and sinew and bone melded into the brighter purposes of design.

Then Sara approached and quickly reached a hand to my face.

"You're clammy and can barely catch your breath. This was a bad idea. Back to bed."

"I feel fine," I said.

"How about if I stay with you?"

"Is that a bribe?"

"A promise."
"Make me milkshakes?"
"If that's what it takes."
"Keep me warm."
She smirked. "It's ninety degrees out."
"We'll turn the air conditioning to sixty."
"Deal," she said.

~ * ~

I pulled and reviewed nearly fifty pieces. Some I was able to dismiss offhand. Others would need reworking, but I could do it in relatively short time. I settled on thirty, so Mrs. Felker would feel useful.

Some were new, the paint nearly tacky. Others were ten years old. I looked for some sense of continuity, but didn't find much. One was a predecessor to *Night Sky* showing a horrible storm at sea, this time with a ship. Others were calm, even outwardly serene, like a revamped *Forest Glen* with far more muted colors and a faceless young woman holding a Smith's blue butterfly. Hands were hidden in its wings, hands-within-hands.

I let her whittle them down to twenty. The last was one of children gathering shells. She studied it closely.

"This is new."

"You're right."

"The little girl here. She has these pale lines on her arms, but the rest is tanned. What does that mean?"

The girl was Karen, the lines where the braces had been. "I just missed the color a little. Want me to redo it?"

Her gaze remained fixed. "No. I don't know what it is, but it's just right." She looked up. "I would ask how many more you have like this, but you wouldn't tell me. And if you did, I'd probably have a heart attack."

I smiled. She discarded the storm, opting instead for a view of the cove from Lover's Point, a slow, steady rain falling on the water below, a reflection of the sun shining through the clouds.

"What shall we call it?"

"How about *Paolo's Rock*," I said.

She gave me an odd look for a moment. "Done." She put the painting aside. "You're getting better, David, and that's scary."

"Why?"

"You're still a young man. What's going to happen when you're fifty? Or seventy?"

I hadn't thought about the future. I didn't even know the origin of my skill as an artist. I was aware of its focus but not its cause. My ability wasn't just from the music. My art wasn't just the practice or the education. It wasn't even the compulsiveness.

Perhaps everything we are to be is contained within us from the time we become self-aware and simply lies dormant until the motions of time awaken it, and us to it. Maybe Maggie was right. We always have a better self inside longing to be.

She called a week later. "Rothschild's is offering a three million dollar advance," she said. "Shall I accept?"

"By all means," I said.

~ * ~

It was one of the newer Volkswagen Beetles, the same yellow as her old one had once been. I'd left it in her parking space at the clinic with the keys in the ignition and a card under a windshield wiper.

For all your stitchin' without any bitchin'.
The National Federation of Careless People.

~ * ~

I got up from her bed. She was sound asleep. I didn't fully understand why, but I think she derived a sense of equity when we shared her bed and not just my own. I quietly got ready to leave. The time was well past midnight, but she had to get up at five, and I had too much energy to sleep. I needed the smell of night in my nose.

Highway 1 was black, but I had the windows down and the air clothed me. The humidity was low, and I could feel the wind without summer stickiness.

For the first time in my life, every element of my existence seemed to be in sync, and all due to her. She had penetrated every aspect of my life, and I loved everything about her.

I loved her face, its sharp angles and big eyes.

I loved her friendship, our conversations about nothing, and how each seemed to have meaning.

I love how she trusted me, how she confided in me, and how comfortable she seemed doing so.

I loved how she believed in my talent without being insincere.

I loved her flesh and the world of comfort it provided.

I loved how she'd brought the fragile expectation of good to me.

I didn't even see the car until it was nearly on my bumper. The driver slowed only in annoyance and blasted the car's horn. I could hear indistinct shouts coming from inside, and I slowed to let him pass.

He didn't even wait until we were through the curve. The driver pulled out and floored it. The car was a heap with no acceleration, and I let off the gas completely to help it along.

We both saw the oncoming headlights at the same time. The passing car swerved over and cut me off. I could feel the anger rise as I slammed on the brakes.

"Hey!" I shouted to a deaf audience. They sped away.

They approached the S-turn too fast. Tires screeched, and the car listed as they slid through the curves. I reached the first as they skated through the last. They couldn't hold the turn, and the rear end skidded across the center line beyond the invisible point-of-no-return. They were out of control.

The car spun recklessly and irretrievably toward the guardrail, tires squalling as the brakes locked. They hit rear bumper first, and the metal gave way. Shouts turned to screams, and my last sight of them was the headlights in my face as they disappeared over the embankment. The accident was over in a heartbeat.

I moved to the narrow shoulder where they had disappeared. The car had skidded down about fifty feet then had launched end-over-end a hundred feet to the rocks below. It rocked with an angry hiss, coming to rest on its crushed top.

I was over the guardrail without thinking. Just like the car, I moved easily at first, then began to slide. I was already in a panic, and getting to the bottom seemed to take forever, though it couldn't have been more than a couple of minutes.

No sound came from inside. An arm protruded from the driver's window, and I swallowed hard as I knelt to take my first look. The interior light flickered and cast odd shadows. I counted four kids, a boy and girl in front and another pair in back. All were bloodied and motionless. The boy in the back lay with his eyes open and his head at an odd angle. He was dead. The girl beside him had a deep gash from the top of her head to her neck. I reached to touch them. Nothing. I couldn't find a pulse.

The music hadn't come. It didn't matter. They were all dead. I reached across the driver to his girlfriend. I couldn't see her very well, but when I withdrew my hand it was covered with blood.

A faint moan startled me. The driver had his face pointed away from me. Somehow he managed to turn his head, and in that queer, yellow light our eyes met.

"Help me," he gasped. "Please."

I called to the music. It seemed disorganized, confused, just as I was disorganized and confused. I calmed myself, but there was no free-spirited note, no mellow warble. The notes rattled around like a restless spirit. I found the chord through the sheer force of my will. Sounds came and went, but the chord held and grew. I took a deep breath and gripped the boy's shoulder. I closed my eyes and shoved it upward.

The chord erupted into a traffic jam of turbulent sound, so loud that I flinched and let go immediately. I forced myself to relax again, letting it reform. Again came that abysmal racket.

I heard a frightened voice. "No. Please. Oh God, not now. Please." The voice was mine.

Then the other voice moaned, the broken boy, as he shuddered once and did not move.

I backed away amid the noise and waited until it subsided. I looked at his broken form and saw only black. I knew I could succeed. I had come so far. I knew of suffering and loss, but I also knew of love and redemption. I gathered myself and began again. The note—sputtering, the ripple-feeble, the chord-chaotic. I held myself until the music expanded into heavenly oblivion and I was lost in it.

I looked deep into him and saw only darkness, but even so the music grew and surrounded me. I squeezed my eyes tightly together and reached again.

"Work, dammit," I muttered. "For God's sake, work."

The chord flew at me, violently, knocking me aside, raging as I jerked my hands away. It assaulted me even as I stumbled back a few steps, my hands clasped over my ears. I was hyperventilating, my breaths short and furious. I clenched my fists to drive the noise away, but it rampaged against me. I tensed every muscle but could not fend off the rampage. The fight finally drained me into emptiness. I looked skyward and screamed at the top of my lungs, "Why? Why?"

The music died immediately, cowardly, its worst done, and I slumped to the ground.

~ * ~

I looked in the mirror and saw myself as something homely and pathetic, blood to my elbows. I had already taken a couple of sleeping pills and waited for them to kick in. I exhausted the hot water in the shower until no trace of my failure remained, the last pink vestiges flowing down the drain. I let the cold run over my head until I couldn't stand it any longer. I fell into bed unconscious.

I dreamed of an endless red abattoir and black smothering air, of sinuous flesh and splintered bone, of muscle and meat and the smell of rot, of soreness and suffering that had no end, and of a low whimpering that could have been mine.

~ * ~

Sara knew something was wrong. I lied, telling her I needed a few days of uninterrupted work for the European pieces. I didn't know what else to do. I couldn't talk to her. I could barely function.

She deserved better than that. She deserved someone better than me, someone who wouldn't even consider leaving without explanation, but that's where I was. I had to get away. Ten years ago I'd come to this point. Much had changed. Nothing had changed. This had only been a pause—a clever, intoxicating pause.

Maybe I'd just been kidding myself.

I called Mrs. Felker. She knew something was wrong, too, but didn't pry. "I'm going to take off for awhile," I said.

"How long?" she asked.

"I don't know. I'll let you know where I am."

She paused. "This doesn't have anything to do with work, does it?"

I killed someone. Again.

"No," I said finally. "I just need to get away."

"Please, David. Let me try to help if I can."

"I will."

"Take care."

"Yes."

Later the doorbell rang. I really didn't want to face her, but I didn't see how I could avoid it. Getting it over with would be better. I could give her some reason to let our relationship go. Maybe I could keep a straight face long enough to hide how much I desperately needed her.

A man stood at the door. I'd seen him before, but couldn't remember where. He stood away, obviously ill at ease, looking like a middle-aged beach bum. He smiled politely and nodded. Then I remembered. The San Francisco auction. Jack Baird.

"Yes?"

"Sorry to bother you. I don't know if you remember me or not."

"I think so. Jack Baird, isn't it?"

He smiled curiously, and his eyes narrowed. "That's not entirely true," he said softly. "My real name is John Patrick Francis O'Beirne. And I think I'm your father."

Fourteen

I don't remember inviting him in or offering coffee or having him sit at my kitchen table. I remember setting a mug in front of him with such a thud that hot black liquid sloshed in all directions. He patiently wiped it up.

"I know this is a shock," he said. "I knew it would be."

"Then why not leave it alone?" I said tersely.

"I want to know if you are my son."

I moved toward the coffee pot to give my hands something to do. I poured myself a cup but couldn't bring myself to sit. "What difference would it make now?"

"Maybe none. I'm not asking for anything. I just want to know."

"Look. I'm really not up for this right now. I don't know you and don't want to know you. I've got a lot to do."

He nodded. "The last thing I want is to cause problems or reopen old wounds. If you're not my son I'll apologize for troubling you and go back the way I came. But if you are my son, I need to know."

"Why?"

He paused, noticeably uncomfortable again. "I need to ask you a question. Just one. And if you answer it truthfully, I give you my word that I'll leave and never come back."

Something was coming, something I wanted no part of, but at least I would be rid of him. "Ask," I said finally.

He looked at me intently. "David. Do you have any... unusual capabilities?"

An unnatural brew of tension and energy enveloped us.

He had a convertible, and I agreed to take a drive with him. The drive would put us out in the open air and make us both less claustrophobic. I sat quietly at first, watching him. He smiled in a way that seemed to give him comfort, knowing what I did not yet know.

"So," he said. "You've got some... thing. You don't understand it, you don't know what to do with it, you can't talk to anyone about it, and you spend most of your time wishing it wasn't there because it has royally screwed up your life. Close?"

"How did you know?"

He laughed under his breath and shook his head. "The Force is strong in my family."

I stared outward, trying hard to show nothing even as the hair on the back of my neck bristled.

"You see," he continued, "it's genetic. You inherited it. From me. My family. And your mother never knew that because I never told her."

Poor Maggie. "Oh," I said weakly.

"So what is it?" he asked.

"What do you mean?"

"Precognition? Telepathy? Telekinesis?"

My look must have been illuminating.

"There are five or six of these little... aptitudes," he continued, "some stronger than others. Sometimes in combination."

I nodded, still trying to absorb it all.

"So what is it?" he repeated.

I didn't want to answer. I'd begun to stare at my hands, and he'd noticed. I stuffed them between my legs.

"I can... heal."

"Good God," he whispered.

My gaze shot to his, wondering if I'd been duped, if I'd just handed my life to someone I barely knew.

He smiled gently "That's the big one," he said. "The Mother Lode. The Magnum Opus. I've never heard of another healer."

I nearly laughed aloud. "Gee. This must be my lucky day."

~ * ~

We sat out on the deck and sipped beer, letting the darkness overtake us. "How did you find me?" I asked.

"When your work started showing up. The name's not that common to begin with, and it was pretty easy to figure out."

"You recognized my mother."

"Yes. Also the style. Temperamental. Brooding."

I shook my head. "A critic."

"No. You're an Irishman to the gills. You've just never known it before."

I let the subject drop. A million questions, most of which I was afraid to ask. He interpreted the silence.

"I guess you want to know what happened to me."

"For starters."

"My mother—your grandmother—died during that time. I had to leave to take care of family business. By the time I got back, I figured it was too late. And..."

"What?"

He lowered his voice. "Your mother never told me she was pregnant. I called her when I got back, and she told me she wanted to leave things the way they were, and that was it."

A toxic deluge of bile and heartache ballooned inside me, all for the sake of a lonely little boy and a hapless mother. *You could have told me, Mama.* Thankfully, my anger was transient. This stranger represented answers, and I suddenly craved answers. "She told me you were in the Navy," I said finally.

"I was. But I was out by then." He settled back, and I watched the memories form. "I was eighteen. We were between wars at the time so joining up seemed like a reasonable thing to do. Got me away from home. Let me grow up a little. When I got out I went to visit one of my buddies in L.A. One night after supper we were outside, and I heard this beautiful music coming from down the street. A piano. It got to the point where I would make excuses to be outside every night at the same time."

I smiled to myself. "She never stopped doing that. Every night after supper, she would play."

"Well, one night I actually knocked on the door. It was the boldest thing I ever did."

"You stayed in California?"

"I always liked it here. And I had some money saved. I was staying in this old run-down motel. I thought it had a lot of personality and that eventually people would come back. So I bought it. Fixed it up. Put together a couple of packages with travel agents. Bought more old motels. Eventually I did okay."

That had to be only a fragment of the truth. I didn't press it. I'd grown used to living without the whole truth.

I invited him to spend the night. I'm not sure I knew why I did, except that as I watched him, I recognized something familiar. He seemed to be at peace in the dark, eyes closed, listening to the surf below.

"So, if this thing is hereditary..." I offered.

He smiled and lifted his chin to the night air. "Hear that?"

I heard nothing but the familiar sounds I heard every night. "What?"

"The sparrow."

I listened again. A bird song came from the big tree, though barely audible. Birds were always in the big tree.

"Okay."

"It's a female. She's got little ones just about ready to leave the nest, and she's trying to calm them before a hawk comes along. And they aren't cooperating."

"I don't get it."

He sighed. "Neither do I." He weighed his words before continuing. He'd probably never had to explain his power either. "It's like... an aura of sound. No real words. Not language. Just impressions. But I get auditory vibes from every living creature capable of making a sound."

I grinned. "Like Dr. Doolittle."

"Yeah, well, Dr. Doolittle never covered cat sex."

"What?"

"When I was about four I starting picking up basic stuff from animals in the neighborhood. You know, hungry or afraid or sleepy. One night I was in bed, and these two cats decided to exercise their conjugal urges right outside my window. Being only four it was slightly weird."

"I'll bet."

"It got better with practice. And then I began to understand that the whole thing was somewhat... exotic and unpredictable."

I understood perfectly. "And the cats?"

He laughed lowly, then roared like a lion and beat his chest with his fists. I laughed with him. He got up. "I'm going to turn in if you don't mind."

"No. Go ahead."

He paused at the door. "Listen, David. I brought something with me. A sort of family history I've been working on. If you'd be interested."

"Yeah," I said. "I would."

~ * ~

I lay in bed reading. The book was the only connection I'd ever had to my family, and the connection was far greater than I could have ever imagined.

Jack had collected stories going back over two hundred years. People living in virtual obscurity, all sharing something they didn't understand, dared not speak about, often with awful consequences. I found the twisted branches of a peculiar family tree.

One hundred fifty years ago a man named Riley worked in a livery and was said to have an uncanny knack with horses. A distant cousin was rumored to have lifted a millstone from a child's leg without using his hands. My great-great-great-grandmother had thwarted a group of men determined to have her land by telling them their own secret thoughts. A lot of the stories were speculative, but on and on the telling went. On and on came the damaged and the dead. Solitary people living lives filled with imagined punishments for unknown sins.

I had the life's work of a man in my hands. Jack Baird, my father, reaching back from generation to generation to uncover whatever slight bits of truth he could find. I read into the night. I read all the way to the end. The book ended with him. The realization was terrible and suffocating.

I got up and tiptoed down the hall. The door was open. He lay still on his side, facing away from me. I watched for a moment then decided to leave him alone.

"You read it," he said, not a question.

"Yes."

He sat up and looked at me. In the grayness of the room I thought I saw a resemblance.

"Having what you have is the real reason you left, isn't it?" I asked.

"My mother was sick. I told you that."

"But you also knew you were the last—that it could end with you. My God, I'm not even supposed to be here."

"In the first place, there could be others. Some had to have children I couldn't trace. And in the second, I was just a kid, David. Twenty-two years old."

"But you knew. You knew what this—thing—did to people."

"No. I thought I knew what it did to people. But I missed the point."

"What point?"

"That they had lives. Every one of those people made lives for themselves. They loved. They knew what happiness was. Just like everyone else."

"What, life is what you make it?"

"Maybe."

"If you really believed that, you wouldn't have given up on her so easily."

He sighed and fell silent for a time. "You're right, of course. I was a coward. And I know I'm not very good at this. But I would like to see it through if we can."

I wasn't sure anything was possible. Being his son, a son of chaos, was more than I wanted to think about, more than I wanted to deal with at that moment. In the last twenty-four hours all the sour elements of my life had been upended and recast, the results just as muddled.

"Good night, Jack," I said finally.

"Good night," he answered.

~ * ~

Sara sat at her desk, reviewing records. It was the most mundane of her chores, but that was why she liked it. Few life-and-death decisions came from records, and very little bloodletting.

Something struck her as odd. She went back and forth through the logs for every day of the past two weeks. She didn't find what she was looking for. She picked up the phone and called the desk.

"Sharon. You remember Estelle Pauling?"

"Yes."

"There's no record of her chemo for the past couple of weeks."

The nurse repeated the same movements at her terminal. "I'm sure she's been in. Somebody's just missed it."

"Check into it for me, will you?"

"I will."

~ * ~

I'd sent Jack home. We promised to keep in touch. This wasn't an ending for us. I just had too much to digest. A hollow had opened in me deeper than anything I'd experienced since my mother died, and I didn't know what to do, but I'd regained my senses enough to know I wasn't going to run away. I had too much to lose.

I missed Sara terribly. I craved her nearness, her touch, and the desire to focus on something other than myself.

We took a walk along the beach. It was after nine, but the sun still hung on the horizon, and faint reminders of light shone everywhere. Sara walked to relax. I thought the habit was odd, on her feet most of the time, literally running from one calamity to another. She liked to loosen the muscles, allowing all the adrenalin to evaporate.

She was troubled. The sudden, unexplained distance I'd put between us had upset her, but there was no way I could explain. I didn't even tell her about Jack.

"I've been worried about you," she said quietly.

"I know. I'm sorry."

"Can we talk about it?"

"I don't know what to say. You know I spend too much time living inside my own head. I don't know what to do about that. I guess the sad truth is I'm a creature of habit, and I don't adapt well to changes, even the ones that are actually good for me."

"Uh-oh."

"Uh-oh what?"

"Well, aren't I one of those changes?"

I didn't answer right away. "You are the best thing that ever happened to me."

She turned and sank into my chest, urging me to pull her in. "I need to be close," she whispered.

"Me, too."

"Are we okay?"

"I want us to be. More than anything."

"Full-steam ahead?"

"How about slowly but surely."

"Past this bump in the road?"

Oh, my beautiful girl. How could I possibly tell you?

"Yes."

She seemed satisfied, then asked suddenly, "David, do you think of us as permanent?"

At last, the complete truth. "Every moment of every day."

~ * ~

Sara fixed her blouse but still sat on the examining table. She was calm by practice, but really hated being on this end of things. Tom Morgan had been her GP since she was a kid and was semi-retired now. After a few moments he came in with a file, smiling.

"I really appreciate this, Tom."

"Always a pleasure."

She smiled weakly. "I've just been feeling a little rundown lately. Wanted to make sure everything was okay."

Actually she'd never felt better. She had more energy than ever before, slept well, a good appetite, strong immune system. The changes unnerved her, like the rally she'd seen in the dying just before the end. Maybe she was just a hypochondriac.

Dr. Morgan looked through her file again, a puzzled half-grin on his face. "I thought I remembered pneumonia when you were about ten."

"Yeah."

"Also some post-pubescent fibroids, some tubal scarring even."

She was worried now. "Yes?"

"Well, I don't get it."

"What?"

"There's no evidence of any of this."

"I don't understand."

"Neither do I. There's no scar tissue on the lungs or the uterus. No fibroids or abnormalities at all. There's not even any viral residue. In short, you have the body you were born with."

Fifteen

Jack kept a boat docked just south of Mendocino. When he called and invited me up for a couple of days I found myself eager to go. I was still ill at ease with myself, and I looked forward to being away.

I found the slip in a maze of floating timber and walked down the dock, bag in hand. A thirty-six-foot cabin cruiser tied there that told me I was in the right place. On the stern, painted in faded gold letters was the name. *S S Maggie*.

He was ready to shove off, and we did so without a lot of conversation. I stood near him and watched as he piloted. He smiled unconsciously and peered out into some purview he did not share, and I was content with only the low rumbling of the engine. The sea rose in three-to-four-foot swells, but the sky was clear, and I quickly became accustomed to the cadence as we surged forward. The sun was high, and we ran for over an hour before we stopped. I could still see landfall like a scale model in the distance.

"Ready for some lunch?" he asked.

I nodded. "How far out are we?"

"Twenty miles or so."

We dropped anchor and moved astern to a round table and chairs. He fetched us each a sandwich and a beer. I sat with my feet propped up looking westward into the remote expansiveness before me. My muscles unwound.

"You really love it, don't you?" he asked.

"What?"

"This," he pointed.

"Yeah. I guess I do."

"You know why?"

"You mean other than all that womb psychobabble?"

He chuckled. "Yeah."

I shook my head.

"Because the land of our ancestors is surrounded by water."

"You ever been there?" I asked.

"No. Want to. At least once before I die. I think it's the source."

I knew what he meant. "Was it your mother?" I asked.

He beamed. "She was a partial telepath. Like me, but with people. Usually the most powerful thoughts people didn't shield. I used to call her Old Elephant Ears, which is one of the reasons I joined to Navy—to get away from home. You can imagine what it's like to be really ticked off and know she heard every evil thought."

"I can imagine."

He settled. "She was a trip, though. She'd catch somebody thinking something they would never want anyone to know and—you know, tip her hand a little. She was a devout Catholic and dragged me to church. One time we were coming out, and the old priest was there greeting people as they left. I was just a kid. And ahead of us was this girl who was built like the Taj Mahal. Well, the poor guy couldn't help but watch after her for a second. So after my mother shakes his hand she bends closer and whispers, 'Yes, she does have an ass just like Betty Grable.'"

I laughed. Jack laughed, too, and I knew he enjoyed talking about things he'd never had the chance to talk about before.

"So she knew about it all."

"Well, not in scientific terms. She didn't know it was hereditary, specifically. She thought it was an act of God. She always thought it was a blessing. You don't know how many times I wished I had her faith."

"Mom was the same way. She always believed it was a gift."

"It's been really tough for you lately."

I'd shared the episode with the kids in the car. I didn't feel like reciting my entire life history, but I'd told him that much. "Still hard to cope," I said. "Don't know what to do."

"Yeah, it truly is a cosmic pisser." He took a swig. "I'll tell you one thing. I'm glad this happened."

He was talking about us. "Me, too," I said.

He raised his can of beer to me. "To new relations."

I responded. "And absent loves."

His expression drooped. Maybe I'd poked him deliberately, but I felt badly about it afterward.

"Absent loves," he said softly.

We locked eyes for a moment. He'd been at the same threshold as I was all those years before and had turned away, just as I was prone to do, and had lived with regret all this time.

"To who we are," I said finally.

He smiled genuinely. "To who we are."

~ * ~

By late afternoon we were still talking. Bit by bit we came to an understanding, though we didn't voice it. We needed each other.

Jack had never married and had only been serious about one other woman, and that had been nearly twenty years ago.

"She had six cats," he joked.

I had just begun telling him about Sara when he suddenly turned an ear to the wind. I could feel his excitement.

"What is it?" I asked.

"Whales," he said. "Let's go."

We gave chase. The pod was small, six or eight gray whales. And as we caught them and steadied our speed, they surrounded us, matching us knot-for-knot. I moved starboard, watching as the long shadows torpedoed up and down with deft agility, occasionally blowing an airy mist before dipping down again.

Jack cried out above the engine's noise, startling me. I looked to find him in absolute rapture, pointing and shouting at me.

"It's you!"

I held a hand to my ear, not understanding.

"They know you!"

Then I understood, at least in part. This was part of the pod that had beached itself. I looked closer to see if my friend was among them, but couldn't tell one from the other. The boat slowed, gradually gliding down. To my surprise the whales also stopped, circling the boat, blowing greetings before diving again.

Jack was breathless, his face red with excitement. "They recognize you. How?"

"Long story," I said.

"One of them keeps calling to you."
"How do you know that?"
"He has a name for you."
"Really? What?"
"Hands."

As I looked Jack pointed. Lolling with the sun glistening off his gray belly was my friend. I looked back to find Jack stripping down.

"What are you doing?"

"We've been invited to join the pod." Naked, he dived in. I was caught up in the moment. I pulled off my shirt and shorts and dived in, too.

The water was still cool, and no sooner had I begun to paddle around to get my bearings than I felt an immense movement beneath me. The whale rose, taking me on his back. Startled but exhilarated, I lay flat, and he submerged with me hanging on for dear life. He didn't go very deep. Maybe he knew I was vulnerable. But I opened my eyes to the salty sting of his world, and even through the blur I could see the entire pod in eternal dance. They hovered vertically, like living monoliths, like great extraterrestrial birds in gray-green sky. Jack moved from one to the other, looking like some mutant frog.

The music came like an awakening kiss, and I looked to see that all the whales glowed green-white within. Just as well. I closed my eyes and stroked the beast beneath me, committing only my frail and mortal affection through my fingers. Oddly, each swam by in succession, and my hand glided along, one after another.

The encounter had brought a portion of healing for me, too. I had been renewed a little. Whatever else might come, I could not deny there was fortune and possibility and unspeakable beauty in the world, and I'd been lucky enough to taste some of it. Then he took me to the surface and the moment was over. The pod gathered and swam away, and Jack swam over to me.

"We've been invited to come along," he said.

"A tempting offer," I answered. "Maybe next time."

"Oh yes," he said.

We anchored near a small atoll for the night. The sunken island gave us just enough shelter from the tide. We sat aft, eating boiled shrimp and drinking too much beer, still basking in the delight of our afternoon romp. The stars were out, and I was sitting on an old lounger tilted far enough back to watch the sky. Jack sat on a stool watching me watch the sky.

"You know, something odd about whales," he began, "dolphins, too."

"What?"

"They're mammals."

"Yeah?"

"Well, once upon a time, all those eons ago, they crawled out of the sea."

"So?"

"They went back. I wonder why."

"Maybe the land they were on got covered up."

"Maybe. Still, if the human race ever did lay waste to itself, they would probably be the most sophisticated animals to survive. Theirs would be the next evolution. The thought comforts me."

"Me, too," I said, lifting my bottle. "To the next evolution."

He raised his bottle then looked at me thoughtfully. "I guess you know you're going to have to try to talk to her eventually."

"Sara?"

He nodded.

We let a melancholy silence settle beneath the breeze. Wistfulness was our shared nature, but from different perspectives: ruefulness for him, a harbinger for me, certainty for neither of us.

"How do I do that?" I said quietly, after a moment.

"Throw yourself at her feet and beg her to never leave you, I guess."

I took a drink. "Good plan."

~ * ~

I was sitting with Sara at a table of an outdoor Italian bistro in town. Throngs of people were moving to and fro, ducking in and out of the heat, but I didn't care. I was talking nonstop.

"We were lost, and we both knew it. Jack wouldn't admit it, even though we could've been halfway to Hawaii. He just stood there, looking out the whole time. And all he says for the next hour is 'We're okay. We're okay. We're okay', and I was freaking out."

Sara watched me without recognition and without levity, still upset.

"I'm sorry if I caused you concern," I said apologetically.

"Concern? Some guy shows up on your doorstep after thirty years, and you just drop everything and take off without a word? Why would that concern me?"

"I know. I should've told you."

"All you've done today is talk about him."

"He's interesting."

"Well, he hasn't exactly been what you'd call reliable now, has he?"

"No. We just seem to have a lot in common."

"That's what I'm afraid of."

"It's not like that."

"Okay, so maybe I'm not being reasonable about this. Maybe I'm being possessive and paranoid and overly emotional and a couple hundred other perfectly normal things. But you scared me, David, and I don't like being scared."

"I made a mistake."

"You disappeared. And not just physically. You vanished inside, and I don't know how to handle that."

"I'm sorry. I've been alone a long time. I've still got some really bad habits, but I'm working on them."

"Is that all it is?"

"What do you mean?"

"If that's all it was, I think you could talk to me about it."

"What else would it be?"

"I don't know—it's like you're another person some of the time. In so many ways it's like I don't know anything about you. Not really."

I nodded. For the first time I wanted to find the words to tell her. "Look. There's some old stuff. Stuff I've been trying to resolve for a long time. I didn't want it to be an issue. I wanted us to have a clean slate."

"There can't be a clean slate until I'm part of the process." She looked away.

I clasped her hand with my fingers. "Can you just trust me for a little while?"

She faced me. She wasn't satisfied, but she finally reached and gripped my hand.

"Yes," she said. "Whatever else, I do trust you."

~ * ~

She punched in the numbers and waited. He answered on the fourth ring.

"Hello, Mr. Pauling? Dr. Rembert at MCM. I'm calling about Mrs. Pauling. She hasn't kept her therapy appointments, and I'm worried about her. Is she okay?"

The line went dead.

"Hello? Hello? Mr. Pauling? Hello?"

She slowly put down the phone. He had hung up on her.

~ * ~

She drove at a crawl, looking for the address, not believing what she was thinking. The day was still early, the sun barely peering out over the mountains. The night had been restless, her subconscious a medley of nonsense. The event at the conference in San Jose. Her sudden perfect health. His secrecy. Common denominators. *Magic.* She inwardly chided herself. *This is ridiculous. There's no possible way he...*

...She found the house and slowed to a stop. An involuntary shiver ran up her spine as she got out of the car and went to the door. She knocked. No one answered. The car was gone. She stepped off the porch, relieved. She'd let her imagination run wild, that's all. Then she heard it. Humming.

She walked toward the back of the house. She rounded the corner and froze. Mrs. Pauling was on her knees, working in a flowerbed, humming "Amazing Grace". She wore a floppy hat, and her face was hidden. Her clothes hung loose and baggy. But unmistakable energy and fluidity showed in her movements. This was not someone who was terminally ill.

She turned, startled at first. Sara saw the impossible truth in eyes bright and clear, flesh pink from the sun, breaths free of disease. A transparent calm surrounded her as she turned away and resumed her digging.

Sara approached without speaking, suddenly knowing what she did not want to know, what she could not fathom, her mind clattering with the unthinkable.

"Mrs. Pauling?" she said weakly.

The old woman stopped but did not look around. "Do you know him?" she asked gently.

Sara could barely squeeze out the word. "Yes."

"Then leave him be." And she started digging again.

Sixteen

He was out with Jack for a couple of hours, but his absence didn't matter. She was on a raw edge. It wasn't as if she was breaking in. She had a key, but she still felt like an intruder.

She opened the door and closed it behind her. She called out to be safe. "David?" No response came. The house was dark and empty except for the ghosts she had come to find. She didn't know exactly what form they would take, but they were there.

She put her purse and keys on a table against the wall. Above it her portrait hung in a place of honor. She couldn't look at the painting without smiling. Pangs of guilt rippled through her, but she kept telling herself her love was stronger, her love demanded the truth.

She knew where he would keep his secrets. She went directly to the studio and flicked on the light. She nearly tripped over a drop cloth. A clean canvas rested on an easel. Flat file cabinets lined the walls. She went to the first. They were all works-in-progress, too accessible and too new.

She searched the room again, trying to think as he thought. There. Behind the most remote wall of files. Not easily accessible, not used frequently. This one was a smaller file. She opened the top drawer. Inside she found a painting of his mother, how she must have looked near the time of her death, her auburn hair knitted with gray, her eyes small but focused, the portent of a smile.

Next was a little girl, curly brown hair and freckles across her nose. She sat on a bicycle beneath a tree on a neighborhood street, but so empty-eyed, haunted. The portrait was disturbing.

She moved downward, backward in time, across the imprints of his life, images familiar and unfamiliar, and less revealing except for the evolution of his skill. She found an image of a little dog, crude but recognizable, leaping so that it perpetually hovered in mid-air.

Only a single drawer remained, and a single piece rested there, facedown, wrapped in paper and sandwiched between two squares of cardboard. She gently pulled the canvas from its place and held it up.

The subject was a boy, his blank face a picture of manifest gloom. Disembodied hands floated luminous against the dark. She understood their power and life, and she thought she understood the pain and confusion of such potency. Her tears came unbeckoned. She pored over the painting for a long time before putting it away.

"Oh, David," she whispered.

~ * ~

Her car was in front of the house when I pulled up. Sara's presence was a nice surprise. But when I went inside the rooms were dark and there was no sign of her.

I found her on the deck in the farthest corner, standing so still the shadows nearly concealed her. Something was wrong. I wondered if another patient she had gotten to know had died.

"Sara?"

She turned but didn't move, her voice strangely detached. "I used the key. I hope you don't mind."

"Of course not. That's why I gave it to you." I moved toward her, but stopped in the center. I didn't know what, but something warned me to keep my distance. "What's wrong?"

She shook her head and laughed lowly. "Nothing. Actually everything is perfect."

"I don't understand."

"Well, I'm past thirty. I've always been relatively healthy, but there's some wear-and-tear. You can't avoid it."

"Are you sick?"

She took a step toward me, a step into a coil of light, and she wore a strange smile that part of me perceived as a threat. I took an involuntary step backward. She stopped.

"I'm not sick. I'm perfect."

"That's good, isn't it?"

"It's not good, David. It's impossible."

"I don't understand."

Her gaze was so penetrating I shivered beneath it. "You did it, didn't you?"

"Did what?"

She stroked her torso from shoulder to waist with the backs of her fingers. "This."

"You're not making any sense."

"Remember the day we went to San Jose?"

My head throbbed. "Yeah?"

"Something happened to a group of psychiatric patients."

"So?"

"I think you did it."

I mustered whatever strength I had left into my voice. "This isn't funny, Sara."

She paused and looked away. And when she looked at me again, her eyes glistened. "David, I've seen Mrs. Pauling."

I crumbled, fading into nothingness without moving. I looked into the face of my redemption knowing now the truth could not be avoided, and part of myself I did not recognize spoke, barely above a whisper.

"I wanted to tell you. I didn't want it to happen this way."

The confirmation seemed to deaden her, as if the space between us had become a void. "My God," she said numbly.

"Listen to me, Sara. We'll talk about this. But right now I want you to get in your car and go home."

"You know I can't do that. You have to tell me."

I turned away, vainly hoping she would simply give up and leave. I could feel her eyes upon my back. The first wave of temper crested. So much virulence. So much disaster.

"When I was a kid I'd walk around with my head in the clouds, thinking I was special—that I'd been singled out for something important."

"Important? David, this is incredible."

I scoffed. "No. It isn't. You can't imagine the utter helplessness. That sick... evil."

"I don't understand."

Tears formed, and I couldn't stop them. "I can't control it. Sometimes it works and sometimes it doesn't, and I never know which until it's too late. People die, and there's nothing I can do."

"Oh, David."

A lifetime of sorrow pooled inside me and threatened to spill over. I didn't want her to see me like this. Without thinking, I was off. Down the steps, across the yard, and recklessly down the slope, tears hot and sticky on my cheeks. I heard her call after me. "David!"

I ran without care, just as I wept without care. I ran across rocks and crevices I feared in daylight, tempting the worst. I ran until my feet reached sand, sinking into it. I began to walk, my breath heaving, fighting for control. I stopped beneath an overhanging rock, the surf pummeling against it. I tried to calm myself, desperate to clear my head.

A few minutes later she was behind me. I didn't even have to look around. I was afraid to look around.

Still breathless, I began. "When I was about ten years old a little girl in our neighborhood got hit by a car. I tried as hard as I could, but I just couldn't make it work. So she died."

"It wasn't your fault."

I turned, daring to face her, goaded by the absurdity of it all. "Of course it was. Somehow, deep down inside me, I must have wanted her to die. That's the only explanation."

"I don't believe that. You were just a kid with this extraordinary thing you didn't understand, and there wasn't anyone around to help."

I began to tremble, and my voice cracked from the strain. "My mother tried. Even she knew how terrible it was."

"She told you that?"

I lowered my face. "I was away at school when she had the stroke. Naturally I was frantic. But then it started to make sense. This was the payoff, you know. Years of being scared to death, and I finally had a reason for it all. I was the only one who could do something about it."

"And she died before you got there."

"She knew!" I cried. "She knew for months she could die. She didn't even tell me about it!"

"Maybe she wanted control of her own destiny."

"No! She was afraid I'd kill her!"

She stepped forward and gently touched my shoulder. "Maybe she was afraid that having you try and fail would kill you."

The tears flowed freely again, and there was nothing I could do to stop them. The walls of ruthless memory threatened to collapse in upon me. I tried to look at her. She watched without fear or reservation, her love anchored in something I couldn't fathom.

She reached for me. All my sorrow swelled to the breaking point. I couldn't stop the inevitable. I really didn't want to any longer. I clutched her with all my strength, and the flood of emotion flew from me.

"It hurts, Sara! God, it hurts so much."

I wept so hard I shook, shook until I could shake no more. She never let me go.

~ * ~

On the walk home I told her about Jack, and she understood why the connection was important to me. I told her how she had inspired me, told her all about Karen, about the people in the store, and how I had tried to make peace with the music. Finally, I told her about the kids in the car. She knew about the accident. She'd been on duty when they were brought in. My emotions were still untenable, and I still felt exposed, but she kept her arm around me the whole way.

"I understand the fear. I understand the guilt. I can only imagine how painful it's been. But you have to know that you're so close now."

"To what?"

"To making sense of it all. Having some peace about what you have. Look, you know how it works. Now you know why. You can even work out the who and the when if you choose to. All that's left is the what if."

"That's a lot."

"I know it is. But you have to admit, a part of you wants this, maybe even needs this, or else you wouldn't have tried at all." She paused. "Something important is at stake here."

"My sanity?"

"Your soul."

~ * ~

We were lying in bed, limbs entangled. She kept caressing me, trying to keep me relaxed. My thoughts were reckless blurs, but I loved her for her effort.

"I'm curious," she whispered after a time.

"What?"

"Mrs. Pauling."

I smiled a little with the recollection. "She was so sick. She thought I was a ghost. She didn't even know what was happening."

"She knew. She warned me off."

"She did? Amazing."

"So why?"

"She was important to you. I didn't want you to feel that everything you had done was in vain."

"Thank you."

"You're welcome."

"David?"

"Huh?"

"The kid who was driving that car is still alive."

~ * ~

The Regional Trauma Center was a series of low-slung concrete buildings as austere as its name. Hardly a window was uncovered, and expressions were subdued, inside and out. Sara took the lead. I fed off her strength.

"He's been comatose since the accident, and he'll have someone with him constantly. But they have to move him for a scan. It'll just be one person. That's the best chance you'll have."

I nodded absently.

"You don't have to do this. We can go back."

I thought for a moment. "No."

"Look, I know this might sound stupid, but there is a trick I learned when I started the surgery program that might help."

"What?"

"Try to imagine that it's something commonplace, that it's not a life-and-death situation."

"Like what?"

She paused. "Remember how we met?"

I smiled. "You and that old car."

"Well, this kid has a flat tire, David. And you're the first guy up the road."

~ * ~

A nurse and attendant moved the limp form on a gurney down the corridor. Bandages swathed his swollen head, and massive yellow-purple bruises covered his face. As they neared the service elevator the nurse veered away. The attendant stopped and pushed the button.

Suddenly from around the corner came a loud crash, the sound of objects falling to the floor. The attendant looked toward the corner. Dr. Sara appeared, white coat and badge, looking very agitated.

"I need a hand here. Stat."

The attendant shook his head. "I can't. I—"

"Now!" she barked. "He's not going anywhere." Then she disappeared around the corner.

The attendant looked worriedly at the boy and then grudgingly moved toward the corner. He saw a pile of empty food trays in disarray on the floor. He looked up the hallway but saw no sign of the doctor. He scowled. Picking up scattered equipment wasn't his job, and the mess wasn't that urgent.

He moved back around the corner. The gurney was gone. He ran toward the elevator. "Damn!"

I was in the elevator with the boy. I'd pushed the express button to the top floor. I figured I had about thirty seconds. My hands were sweating. I had to make a connection but didn't know what it could possibly be.

Our last meeting had been a disaster.

He looked different in the light, and imagining all he had left to do wasn't hard.

He would go to school somewhere and not study enough, but he would also learn what was his to learn—things he would never forget. He would come to understand discipline and hopefully find a vocation he loved.

He would work, find the routine unbearable at times, but also find those rare moments of enlightenment that would help him make his mark. He would learn the satisfaction of using his own wits and resources.

He would fall in love and fail. He would fall in love and succeed, at least for a time. He would have children and become too much like his own father. He would feel invincible and learn all too soon his own frailties.

But more than this, he would find his life was to do with as he pleased, to function and falter beneath the incorruptible cause of choice, and he had so many more choices to make. Anything less was unacceptable. He would live.

"Okay, kid," I said softly. "Let's do it right this time."

I closed my eyes and reached my hands toward his face. The note came on command, restless at first, wavering, but then gentle into the chord. It hovered momentarily, as if waiting. I waited, too, until the fear subsided. I urged the chord upward.

It soared effortlessly, and I rode upon its wings. The hum of the elevator and my own breathing faded into the music. I glimpsed all the dark sores inside him but ignored them. I touched him. I became lost in the music as it ebbed through. Oddly, I found myself hoping some part of him would remember. And perhaps years from now, he would sing an unknown melody to his own child as he rocked him to sleep.

~ * ~

The attendant had summoned the nurse, who had summoned a doctor. Even with the prospect of losing his job, he wouldn't lie. He told them exactly what had happened and pushed the elevator button again, as if his agitation would hasten it.

Finally they heard the distinct rumbling of the approaching car. The light overhead blinked, and the bell chimed. Three sets of eyes moved in unison toward the doors, preparing to dart inside.

The doors parted, and the gurney was there. The attendant sighed with relief and began to roll it out. Even before the bed stopped the doctor was moving to the boy's eyes, penlight in hand.

Suddenly the boy's eyelids fluttered and opened by themselves. The three leaned backward in surprise. The kid squinted, his eyes sensitive to the overhead light. Groggily, he tried to focus.

"Where am I?" he muttered.

Seventeen

I didn't work for awhile, at least not with the same ferocity. I hadn't quit, of course—far from it. I'd already selected the next twenty pieces to whip into shape. I just wanted to take a break. Oddly enough, I began spending more time at Maggie's piano, with apologies to Monsieur Claude.

Sara met Jack. The three of us had a bond we never verbalized. We didn't need to. Jack would regale us with stories of his life. Often he would speak of my mother. Sara got to know her. Jack and I got to know her again.

Sara and I spent a lot of time together, most of it doing nothing. She never broached the subject of my hands unless I brought it up first. I found myself initiating discussion of the music more and more, and she would listen patiently as I tried to describe my experiences from beginning to end, and the events that had shaped me. Occasionally she would make suggestions and then give me time to digest them.

Whatever lived inside me had grown during its hiatus. She taught me the basics of meditation so I could distance myself from the music and find more of what I was apart from it.

Above all, we were content. I rested well. We loved well. I was even a little lazy. Most of all I enjoyed letting my mind wander over the landscape of my life without agonizing over every exposed root and fallen limb. And the music became a less urgent reminder of its presence within me.

Still, we kept to ourselves most of the time. Jack kept his distance unless invited, always asking if it was a bad time whenever he called. He called often, and I didn't discourage him. He seemed lonely at times, and I understood. He'd never maintained any kind of intimate relationship, and we had started to become an odd little family.

During late August, near summer's end, we went for a walk at twilight, low tide. Autumn would be upon us soon. Ours was not the same as a New England autumn, but the nights would grow cooler, the sea would change, and the hardwoods would burn in golds and reds.

I had a habit of picking up the debris that washed ashore below my house. Cleaning the beach was an utterly futile act, but I liked the exercise. Sara was perched on a nearby rock, peeling an orange and dodging the gulls as they swarmed, waiting for a treat.

I began talking, just thinking out loud more than anything. "You know, that back bedroom's just wasted space. It could be made into an office or study or something like that."

She looked at me without expression. "Yeah?"

"And I've really got more room than I know what to do with. There's plenty of privacy."

She smiled to herself. "Yeah?"

I looked at her and saw the smugness. "You aren't going to help me out here, are you?"

She shook her head and took a bite of orange. "You're doing fine."

"So what would you think about moving into my house?"

"You mean like, to stay?"

"Of course to stay."

She paused. "I don't know."

She was teasing me. I dropped the bag and walked over to her, putting my hands on her waist. "What don't you know?"

"How serious you are."

I adopted my most deadpan expression and lowered my voice. "Really serious."

"Really?"

"Really."

"Yeah?"

"Yeah."

"You and me. Under the same roof."

"Yes. Let's do it."

"Right here on the beach?"

"Don't be a wiseass."

She slid off the rock and into my arms. "Come on, Buster. Pay up."

I laughed and shook my head. Suddenly she pushed me over, and I fell backward onto the sand with her on top of me. The sand was cold and damp, but I didn't care. She bent to kiss me.

"I can see the headlines now," she whispered. "Local physician accosts artist on beach."

I pulled her close. "I won't press charges."

~ * ~

Almost like criminals, we moved her in the middle of the night, but it was the best time for us both. She was still working a lot, and I was beginning to have a hard time sleeping without her. I set up an office for her in the back room and had her private number transferred.

We settled into a routine. I would cook and do laundry, and she would work and rest and look after me. And every day we would sit and talk for at least an hour about everything and nothing that had only to do with us.

I hadn't seen Mrs. Felker since our last phone conversation, and I owed her an explanation. I didn't know what I would say, but I wanted to reassure her.

On Sunday afternoon her gallery was closed. I found her in her office, working at the antique writing table with one leg propped up in a guest chair. She smiled up at me and stopped working. She grimaced as she withdrew her leg for me to sit down.

"Damn knee," she muttered.

"What is it?" I asked.

"Bursitis," she answered. "A word of advice. Avoid getting old at all costs."

I sat, not wanting her gesture to be in vain.

"Actually, I'm looking forward to it."

She looked at me intently. "Are you now?"

"Yes."

"So, how are you?"

Despite her casual tone, it wasn't a casual question. "Much better."

She nodded. "Sara came in last week. Looking for a gift for someone. She told me about Jack."

I didn't see any harm in allowing her to believe that his appearance was all there was to my silence. It seemed enough. "Yeah, that's pretty strange."

"Maybe it will be good for you."

"I think so."

She paused. "Okay to talk a little shop?"

"Sure."

"I wanted to talk to you about what kind of structure to set up with all this new attention. How you want to proceed, how many pieces you want to release, that kind of thing."

She was being careful around me, and that wasn't like her at all. Maybe my absence had upset her more than I'd realized. "You handle that. I don't care."

She sat upright and looked at me almost apologetically. "I've known you a long time now. I don't think you know what this association has meant to me."

"Me, too."

"Then you have to know there are scores of people in this business who can do a lot more for you than I. You're in the big leagues now, and it would bother me tremendously if you ever felt short-changed."

Ah. "You want to quit?"

"God no. But it wouldn't hurt for you to examine your options."

I shook my head. "I don't care about that."

"You should never let loyalty stand in your way," she said.

"It's not just loyalty. I like having someone care about what I do and letting me do what I do. If you're worried that it's getting too big, hire somebody. You can afford it."

She smiled genuinely. "I might just do that." She shifted her position, and in doing so must've aggravated her knee because she flinched and lifted her foot off the floor. I reached down, took it, and gently rested her heel on my leg.

I know the familiarity surprised her. She knew I didn't like physical contact. In all the time I'd known her we'd probably actually touched fewer than ten times. She even reddened, but didn't resist. "You don't have to..."

"Let your leg rest," I answered.

Her knee was so swollen that there was no shape to it except for a dome of red and tender flesh. I put my hands thumbs-first just below the injury, careful not to apply any pressure, barely touching the lower edge.

"It's awful, isn't it?" she said.

"Did I hurt you?"

"No. Just when I bend it."

The note began. I pushed it back from force of habit. Then, I called to it, not audibly, of course, but the note came. I told the music what I wanted. Gently. Nothing more than a whisper. No need for clamor, no need to rush. It obeyed. Movement, then to the chord, sweetly like a caress. *Hold now. Wait for me. No need to hurry.* The healing sound lifted so delicately, and I moved my thumbs to both sides of her knee and began to rub very softly in small circles. I did not need to see to know.

All the while I looked at her, smiling, trying to keep her attention on my face. I released the power sparingly, something I'd never tried before. It seeped into her gently.

"Give me back forty years, and you'd be in big trouble," she cracked.

"What about Mr. Felker?" I said. "You wouldn't have wanted to miss him."

She sighed. "He had his moments. God, it's been twenty years. A heart attack at fifty-four. I still remember what he looked like."

"Why wouldn't you?"

"You know what's really odd about all that?"

My massage was nearly unnoticeable. "What?"

"He was old school. Husband, father, provider. He started in real estate back when there wasn't even a bus stop here. He knew what was coming. But he worked all the time."

"Yeah?"

She pointed her chin corner-to-corner. "This was just a lark. Something for me to do when the kids were grown. I didn't care if it worked or not. So naturally it made a profit the first year." She paused. "Didn't matter. He wouldn't slow down. He just didn't know any other way. Two years later, he was gone."

"I know you miss him."

"Well, I never got remarried. Never really wanted to."

It was done. I slowly pulled my hands away while the memories settled. Then she looked at her knee curiously. The flesh was still red and puffy, and would be until the natural processes reacted to the wholeness.

"Better?" I asked.

She eased her heel away from my leg and gingerly touched the floor, keeping her knee rigid. Then she flexed a little, obviously amazed that she could, and could without pain.

"What did you do?"

I wiggled my thumbs. "Acupressure. The Discovery Channel. But I wouldn't overdo it if I were you. It's still going to be tender."

"You never cease to amaze me," she said.

I smiled. "I watch too much TV." Then, impulsively, I bent and kissed her on the cheek.

~ * ~

She had been pensive the last few days, spending entire evenings without saying much, and I didn't know what to make of her unusual mood.

One night, when the wind was up and the sky was overcast, I found her standing at the railing of the deck gazing out into the distance. She was even shivering, but didn't move.

I walked up behind her and put my arms around her. She squeezed her neck back against me but said nothing. I could hear a boat in the distance and listened until it faded away.

"Are you happy here with me?" I asked.

"Yes on all three counts," she said. She turned and nestled into my chest. "Just hold me a little."

"How about I hold you a lot," I whispered.

"Oh yes. Please do."

~ * ~

I'd begun to wonder if the true purpose of memory wasn't to remain fluid along an entire spectrum of experience, waiting dispassionately and with infinite patience for us to recognize its sway and respond to it. Perhaps events truly repeat themselves, playing out time and again until our own evolution allows us to exist farther along the spectrum; perhaps peace exists as a droplet on one end and a river on the other at all times, from the commencement of any memory, revealing more of itself to us as we are able to see it, like the ever-present sun emerging from night, and we are able to harmlessly imbibe it and disgorge it and thornlessly consume it.

There is no such thing as poor timing, only the poverty of recognition.

Any event was shaped by perspective, capable of good or harm, and I could enjoy it or curse it or weather it or do whatever I wanted to do with it, but I had to do more than merely survive every event, or else never partake of anything more than the droplet.

I had a talent and vocation I enjoyed that allowed me to express every part of myself existing along the spectrum, through which I had become prosperous.

I had a friend and a lover who had come to know so much of my life, but who saw the personality and heart apart from that, and together we could grow along the spectrum, and could live together until all the reasons to do so had been exhausted.

I had come to know my father, and that through him I had inherited a strange talent, but a talent to do good to those who had no other options, and that I could not hide from it, and must deal with whatever failings I encountered with something less than grim inevitability.

I did not know what the future would hold for this part of myself, but I had to move among the living and dying without paralysis—perhaps even with no judgment as to which was which. Nothing dies without first having lived—nothing lives without ultimately perishing; nothing in life survives unscathed.

The right to seek wholeness is apportioned the same to all people.

Somehow I would do what I could do.

~ * ~

Many trails crossed through the Los Padres National Forest, one a favorite of mine. I hardly ever went there, but sometimes I needed a contrast to the sea. The trail was only a couple of miles from start to finish, and not the forest primeval, of course, but a nice corridor of trees and the life contained within, and a cloistered place.

I parked and walked. The hour was still early, and a fine haze rose from the undergrowth waiting to be burned away. The bicyclists were out, but not so many yet, and we gave each other room. A group would pass, and then several minutes might go by before I saw another.

In those minutes I found my pleasure. I listened to birds and tried to understand just as my father would. I wished Sara were with me. She was never far from my thoughts, like a coin in my pocket. I fretted about my work. I had recently sketched out a piece with Jack sitting on his boat with his feet propped up, dozing in the sun with a large orange cat in his lap.

I walked from columns of sunlight into shadow and back again, feeling incredibly alive, and, strangely enough, like a whole person.

A rustling in the tall grass just off the path startled me. Mountain lions lived in these parts. I stopped dead, afraid to run. The rustling moved toward me. A flash of black...

A puppy emerged from the brush. It had the head and shape of a Lab but with short hair and an oversized tail that curved back all the way to its head. The pup couldn't have been more than a couple of months old, and was thin and gaunt. It stopped to look at me, cautious at first, but soon wagged its tail, its tongue lolling as it sucked in the cool air. We kept our distance, and I was about to turn back when a couple of cyclists came whizzing by.

The pup nervously jumped aside, skipping out of harm's way by picking up a back leg. I laughed. Providence had a sense of humor.

"Well, boy, this is your lucky day."

I crouched and called to him. At first he just cocked his head at me, but gradually—a step and a pause, another step and another pause—he crept closer. I reached the back of my hand in his direction so he could get a whiff. He craned his neck as far as his head would reach without actually moving any closer. I dropped my fingers to the top of his head, scratching gently. He responded, closing his eyes and shrugging his shoulders. I patted my thigh to see if he would come. He did.

I slowly moved a hand to the offending hip. The music came quickly, to the chord inside a moment. The song moved upward and held. The tips of my fingers barely grazed the dog's fur, and yet I could feel the music working. The healing was becoming more effortless, and I closed my eyes to bring it into focus—and to capture the feeling.

Again I began to see an image but ignored the aura. Instead I concentrated on the music, to find again what I had embraced as a child, before the other, before I had known there was anything else. So much of my life held some deep, heart-breaking disappointment, and I wanted—needed—to clutch and cradle it again, to be salved by its most intimate song, and perhaps finally, to be absolved from the persistent doubt the music had brought to me.

It was there welcoming me, honoring me, loving me. And for the first time in my adult life, I was grateful for the presence.

A few seconds and the task was done. The puppy just looked at me curiously. I waved my hand above his head so he would test the leg. He didn't understand, so I got up and began to back away. He followed, stiffly at first, but without the limp. He seemed less interested in his own health than he seemed interested in me. I moved, and he followed. No matter how quickly I walked, he kept up. I tried to shoo him away, but he bounded back and forth, wanting to play. Finally I was back at my car, and the dog was still there.

He sat on his haunches and looked at me as if asking, 'Now what?' The last thing I wanted was a dog.

He lay quietly on the passenger seat, his triangular head resting on his front paws. "This could be trouble, Lucky," I said. He looked at me. "Dr. Sara can be a pretty soft touch, but both of us may end up in the dog house."

He yipped once in agreement.

I made a bed for him out on the deck until he was housebroken and put his food and water dishes nearby. Sara looked at him vaguely.

"Why Lucky?"

"It seemed to fit."

They stared at each other for a minute until she finally bent down and gave him a good scratch. He obliged by turning onto his back and kicking his leg as she rubbed. I knew the feeling.

She gave me a sideways glance as she patted his head. "Welcome to Bedlam," she said finally.

I had no idea what she meant.

Eighteen

I was standing in the shower rinsing my head. Sara had to work second shift, and we had spent most of the morning exploring the hills north of us, letting Lucky get a run in. Our hills were not the sandy dunes of Southern California. Ours were the rocky knots of stubborn grasses and antiquity. Lucky had been rooting around and found an arrowhead. He'd brought it to her and laid it at her feet. He'd already learned which way the wind blew.

I heard her come in and begin to get ready. Cohabitation brings out levels of intimacy that do not exist otherwise. Sex is not the ultimate intimacy. Sharing a bathroom is.

She stood at the sink washing her face. Steam from the shower covered the mirror in a thin layer. "You're fogging me," she called out.

"What?"

"I said you're fogging me."

I turned down the hot water. "What time will you be home?"

"Late," she said.

"I'll have something for you in case you're hungry."

She began blotting her face with a towel. "Speaking of which," she muttered.

I didn't know if she was talking to me or not. "What?"

"I said I'm late."

"No, you're not. It's only two-thirty."

She smirked at her own reflection. "God, David, you are so slow."

I smiled. I enjoyed her ribbing. Then my smile dropped. I didn't know what she was ribbing me about. Her meaning slowly began to dawn on me, and I turned the shower off and stood there frozen, afraid to move.

"How late?"

"A week or so," she said.

I opened the shower door and watched her in the mirror. She didn't acknowledge me except to throw me a towel over her shoulder. Mechanically, I started to dry off. "What exactly does that mean?" I asked.

"It probably means I'm just a little late."

She was never late. The phases of the moon, the tides, and Sara's menstrual cycle were all certainties of the natural world. "Or?" I asked.

She still hadn't looked at me directly. "Or," she said with a sigh, "we're going to have a little leprechaun or whatever it is that runs in your family. Knowing you he'll probably have pointed ears and walk around saying things like 'live long and prosper'."

I smiled feebly. She nervously busied herself with makeup. Finally, she turned.

"Nothing says we have to go through with it," she said. "If it's true."

"Would you really want this, knowing what you know?"

She paused for a moment. "Yes, David. I would."

"Why?"

"Because it would be a part of us both. Because we know things your parents didn't know."

I thought about all the corruption in the world. Blaming society was a ruse, of course. I could not think long about my own genetic makeup without naming it a defect. She reached to hold me, perhaps so she could no longer see the doubt on my face as much as anything else. I heard her voice, low and calm, believing in a life for us at the far end of the spectrum.

"Tell me the truth. Isn't it really different now—so much better than before?"

You will have so much magic in your life, David.

"Yes," I said. "So much better."

~ * ~

They were lost in an infuriating way, with no real idea of where they were or where they'd gone wrong. He drove the RV tight-lipped and tight-fisted, while she studied the map as if she really did know east from west, north from south.

"I told you that was the road when we passed it," she said.

"You didn't say anything," he grumbled. "Here, give me that."

He swiped at the map, but she pulled it out of reach. "Don't be so grouchy. We've seen some nice scenery."

"I see lines on the road, but no park."

He waited for the right moment and snatched the map away. He sprawled it across the steering wheel, half-watching the road, half-reading the map. He rounded a curve too widely, the tires screeching.

She leaned and tried to get at the map. "Watch where you're going!"

He elbowed her hand away and squeezed wrinkles into the paper. He bore down on the crossroads, his eyes flicking up for a moment. No traffic. He looked back at the map.

The car emerged from behind a ridge, a quarter mile from the intersection. The woman saw it too late. "Carl! Look out!"

Sara was listening to a digitally remastered copy of *Abbey Road*, a newly acquired treasure. *Once there was a way, to get back home...* She was lost in the reverie of new life and a new world, and saw the RV peripherally but ignored it. She had the right-of-way.

The RV made no effort to slow for the stop sign. The monster had already crossed the plane of the intersection before the driver hit the brakes. Much too late.

She turned a split-second before impact. She didn't even have time to think. She uttered a single word.

"David."

The RV plowed into Sara's car at the driver's door, knocking the bug sideways off the road. It skidded through the grass until it hit a rock and overturned, tumbling roof-to-wheels four times before finally coming to rest upside down against a hillside.

The RV lurched to a stop. The woman was hysterical, and the man was white-faced with shock. "Dear Lord, you killed somebody!"

Trembling uncontrollably, he opened the door. "Just shut up, will ya!"

He ran to the car. The glass was shattered, the entire driver's side crushed inward, the broken wreckage sighing in its death throes. The airbag had deployed, pushing the woman out the opening where the window had been. She hung upended from her seat, held in place by her harness, unconscious and limp, her head bleeding profusely.

He ran back to the RV and called up to his wife. "Call somebody! Hurry!" He began to cry. He had seen death in Korea and knew he could do nothing for her but weep.

~ * ~

Dr. Evans worked frantically, muttering to himself. "Fourth through seventh ribs fractured. Blood in the lungs. Spleen's gone. Liver's a wreck. Bleeders everywhere." He looked up to find all eyes frozen upon him. "I said whole blood!" he commanded. "What are you waiting for?"

The gathered watched him as he exited, even though there was bustle all around and much work to do. He approached, weary and careworn, still draped in his bloody gown.

"We've got the bleeding stopped, and she's stable. But we aren't equipped for her head injury. Chopper's been called?"

"Yes, doctor," a nurse replied.

"We'll just have to wait like everyone else."

"Should I call David?" the nurse asked.

He nodded. "Tell him to meet us at the trauma center. She'll be gone by the time he gets here." He paused then, weighing his words. "You know what I meant."

No one answered.

~ * ~

I was in full muse, wondering if I should knock down the wall between the master bedroom and the guest room to put a nursery there. Jack could always use the couch.

The phone rang. I almost let it ring so that I could remain in full muse, but the I.D. read Mid Coastal.

"What did you forget?"

"David? This is Sharon Mitchell from the hospital."

I waited, afraid to breathe.

"It's Dr. Rem—Sara. There's been an accident."

"Oh God. How bad?"

"Serious. We're going to have to move her to the trauma center. You should go there."

"No! Keep her there until I get there. I can—"

"We can't wait, David."

Fear and panic compressed into a bomb and began to tick. "I can help her. It will only take me a few minutes!"

"We've got to evac her. We've got no choice."

"Tell them to wait for me, Sharon!"

"The chopper is on its way!"

Arguing was pointless. I abruptly hung up, swiped the keys, and flew out the door. I was on the road in less than sixty seconds. Even in the dead of night it would have taken me at least ten minutes to make the commute, and this wasn't the dead of night. For the first time in ten years I hated my seclusion.

I sped down the highway, passing a truck on the curve, not caring what damage I did or to whom as long as I made it in time. I downshifted up the hill, pulling sixty-five in third gear, the engine whining with its effort.

All the while a mantra rose, seeming so cruelly familiar, so unnaturally natural. "Hang on for me, Sara. Please. Just hang on. I won't make it without you."

In six minutes I was at the turnoff. Only two more miles, but through development and traffic. I ran the first two red lights I came to, slowing just enough to squeeze through safely. I prayed that a cop would see me and run interference, but it didn't happen. All I got were the looks and gestures that accompany the shrieking of brakes.

I made it into town. Ahead was the last light. Turn right, a half mile, and I would be there. At least five cars were ahead of me, and I had to stop. I pounded my steering wheel in frustration. "Move!"

Then I heard it. I don't know what woke me to the sound except that it was so unusual. It was a rhythmic wump-wump-wump overhead, and I looked to see the air ambulance cruise by. It would be at the hospital in two minutes, have her loaded and away in five. I had run out of time.

I jumped the curb onto the sidewalk. I bumped my way up the cement, dodging signs and poles until I reached the parking lot of the convenience store on the corner. I headed straight across the lot, weaving among a couple of cars, nearly clipping a pedestrian, and shot back onto the road, cutting off a truck. I could hear the blare of his horn as I sped away.

~ * ~

Sara lay unconscious in the unlit room, her swollen head bandaged, a tube in her nose, an IV in her arm. Dr. Evans watched her. She was prepped to go, but he wouldn't move her until the last second. She was still very fragile, and he knew she might not survive the trip. He was paged. He grimly shook his head and left.

~ * ~

I slammed to a stop near the emergency room entrance. A nurse watched me curiously, but said nothing. An ambulance crewman called to me, "Hey, you can't park there!" I ignored him. Behind me I heard it again. The helicopter was moving in for a landing.

I sprinted to the desk. Sharon was there. I could see the worry in her face.

"Where is she?" I asked breathlessly.

"They're getting ready to evac her, David."

"Please, Sharon. Where is she?"

She hesitated. Finally, she pointed. "Trauma three."

I moved quickly. Another nurse appeared at the corner. "Sir. Sir! You can't go in there."

I avoided her and pushed open the door. I stopped short, seeing Sara lying lifeless in the faint light, the sounds of monitors echoing her heartbeat and breath, both surrealistically slow. The sight was agonizing. "Oh, Sara," I whispered.

I knew, of course. This was why I was here, perhaps even what I was born to do. I slowly approached the bed, calling to the music and feeling the note come and mingle with the fullness of love. A slight commotion erupted outside, and someone else entered the room. It didn't matter. I was here. I dismissed whoever it was until I felt a hand upon my shoulder.

"David," he said gently. My eyes never left her, my movement never stopped. "David, let us handle this," he said more firmly. I pushed his hand away, summoning the notes to gather. Then he gripped my shoulders more aggressively, distracting me. "David, you can't..."

I spun suddenly, angrily. He must have understood, at least something, because his expression and tone softened in mid-sentence. "... help her."

Our gazes collided. "Yes I can."

He looked at me curiously but let me go.

I moved to the bed and sat beside her. I smiled a little and touched her cheek beneath the bandages. She didn't look like herself. I took her hand and brought it to my lips. I needed to feel her against my skin. The tears welled, not frightened tears, not tears of loss. Tears of consent to search for an oasis along the spectrum where we two could meet.

I beckoned again, and the music came. The note, its fluttering assembly, the chord. I closed my eyes and leaned forward, allowing my fingers to skate along her temples. The blackness startled me. Nothing but darkness, an abyss of night. I inhaled and lifted my chin to raise the chord toward completeness.

The music slammed downward. I fought to hold it, but my heart floundered, and in its ferocity was a warning: no magic is perfect. I froze for a moment then let go. I was shaking, afraid, overwrought, my love before me in the gray veil of death. I knew I could succeed and did not panic, calming myself with slow, easy breaths, the way she taught me.

There was only one solution. Me.

I began again. The music came, and we spoke to each other as if bargaining, offering assurances neither was certain we could keep.

As the music swelled I reached again.

The noise collapsed in upon me, bombast and terror. I knew then that I had lost everything. No matter what else might come, a part of the music was there to punish and provoke me, to take away every good thing I had ever found.

So I held on.

As if I were holding onto a live electrical wire, jolt after jolt blasted into me. I fought. Harder than I'd ever fought before, in conceit and hatred. The harder I fought, the louder the tumult became. I raged against the chaos, screaming at it voicelessly, matching clatter for clatter, determined to endure until it was done, myself or the music or both. I would not let go.

The roil of storm and the pitch of hell boiled around me, and I felt the violation of every ruptured cell within her. But I did not relent.

Suddenly amid all that pandemonium another part of myself came alive. And I glimpsed her on a distant green hill, the white sky bending near. She seemed so calm, and I was compelled to move toward her. All about me was howling wind and crashing storm, but I continued on. I moved through the maelstrom toward the brightness that surrounded her.

The music stalked me, snapping and snarling. But I no longer fought. My eyes were upon her, and I kept moving—surprised I could, surprised the chaos hadn't torn me apart.

As I neared, I heard it. The music that healed. Faint at first, but even against the clash of its twin it was there—the chord in all its harmony, strong and unwavering and sweet.

The healing music had been there all along, just beyond my reach, just beyond my willingness to seek it out and love it. At first the sound seemed overwhelmed by the other, but not diminished.

So I reached. Hesitantly, at first, but I stretched through the blackness and noise until the tips of my fingers danced in the crispness of green-white sublimity. I began to strengthen, even as it grew, and the music began its slow, steady march into me. Little by little the chord began to replace that hateful racket like dawn erasing the dusk.

The other protested and struggled, but continued to dissolve until all that remained was music so gloriously pure it engulfed me, until the power surrounded us both.

She was before me again, asleep as she had been, my hands perched upon her face, the music overflowing. I gave the gift to her, feeling it move powerfully down my arms, cascading like a spring rain. In slow, hushed pulses the music left me. We were together in the healing miasma, and the light that had encircled the far hill encompassed us. The black had been bleached into gray, and gray mingled with white until we were in the clouds and the songs of angels nurtured us.

She still slept as we were locked in that embrace, and I spoke to her through the music.

You have saved me, Sara. Please come back to me.

~ * ~

Dr. Evans watched, trying to understand such rashness, such morbid attachment. The poor man had lost all sense, clinging to her in such a way, shuddering and moaning under his breath. Perhaps he would never recover. It was a horrible thought.

As he turned away the monitors increased pace. Her heartbeat grew stronger, her respiration neared normal, and the beeping became louder. He leaned toward the bed just to convince himself he was imagining things.

Her eyes flicked open, and he took an involuntary step back. "My God, what..." he murmured.

~ * ~

I heard her groan and finally lifted my hands. I kissed her and realized she was struggling to get her bearings.

"David?"

I smiled through tears. "Sara."

She looked around and realized where she was. "What happened?"

"You had a flat tire."

She slid her arms around me. Dr. Evans stood there in shock and disbelief. "Am I okay?" she asked.

Dr. Evans moved toward her and checked her vitals, his hands quivering a little. "It would seem so," he said after a moment.

She lay back as the doctor and I stared at each other. "What do we do now?" I asked.

He shook his head. "No one would believe this."

"Then there isn't any reason anyone else should know, is there?"

He paused. "No, there isn't."

Sara intervened. "I think I should stay here. Recuperate gradually under Dr. Evans' expert care. Make sure everyone understands the injuries weren't as severe as we thought. Right?"

He gave us a puzzled grin. "Yes. This kind of trauma can paralyze the cortex and make it appear that all sorts of things have happened that haven't... really... happened."

"You'll want to monitor her progress personally," I suggested.

"Of course." He looked at me again, lost in a world he'd never expected to encounter. "We manage to pull this off, I want to have a long talk with you."

To my surprise, I nodded. "Any time."

Epilogue

Seven months to the day after the accident, Sara Margaret O'Beirne was born. She was perfect.

As for myself, I know I am not perfect. Perfection is not even an aspiration, merely an attribution to some higher calling still so unfamiliar to me.

Our lives certainly aren't perfect. Sara still works too much. I still obsess about things too much. We don't get enough sleep these days, and we don't talk to each other as much as we should.

My father is around more often visiting his granddaughter. He sings to her when he doesn't think anyone else can hear.

I find myself looking forward to the night, when my beloved is asleep and I can cradle my daughter to my chest and rock her in a chair that once was my mother's. In the quiet of that hour I talk to her, even if she can't possibly understand. I tell her who I was and who I became. And I tell her of a future none of us knows.

I have not failed since the accident. The clamor still arises at times, but I can summon the golden voice of the other when it does.

We are now a conspiracy of three. Between my wife and Dr. Evans, I have ample opportunity to do what I do.

They honor me with privacy, secrecy, and anonymity, and are always concerned about my state of mind. We travel together to where those afflicted are completely unaware of anyone's presence. I actually think Dr. Evans and my wife enjoy the espionage.

Sometimes I falter and grow weary. Though the nightmares have passed for the most part, I still wake on occasion in the deep of night and realize I am not yet a complete person. But at least I understand what it takes now.

I can heal.

Meet

M. A. Street

M A Street is a published author and produced playwright. He lives in the Upper Midwest with his wife, Donna.

*VISIT OUR WEBSITE
FOR THE FULL INVENTORY
OF QUALITY BOOKS*:

http://www.wings-press.com

*Quality trade paperbacks and downloads
in multiple formats,
in genres ranging from light romantic
comedy to general fiction and horror.
Wings has something
for every reader's taste.
Visit the website, then bookmark it.
We add new titles each month!*